# *Good If It Goes*

# Good If It Goes

## by Gary Provost and Gail Levine-Freidus

*Bradbury Press*        *Scarsdale, N.Y.*

*The authors wish to thank the following people for their comments and advice on the text: Rabbi Harold Roth of Congregation Agudas Achim, Fitchburg, Massachusetts; Rabbi Sidney Shanken of Flanders, New Jersey; and Zev Shanken of Teaneck, New Jersey.*

*Bradbury Press, Inc.*
*2 Overhill Road*
*Scarsdale, N.Y. 10583*
*An affiliate of Macmillan, Inc.*
*Collier Macmillan Canada, Inc.*
*Manufactured in the United States of America*
*10 9 8 7 6 5 4 3 2 1*
*The text of this book is set in 11 pt. Baskerville.*
*Library of Congress Cataloging in Publication Data*
*Provost, Gary, 1944–*
  *Good if it goes.*
  *Summary: Twelve-year-old David, juggling the demands of Shrimp League basketball and preparations for his upcoming Bar Mitzvah, strives to please Kelly, his dream-girl classmate, as well as his ailing grandfather and traditional parents.*
  *[1. Bar mitzvah — Fiction.   2. Jews — United States — Fiction.*
*3. Basketball — Fiction.   4. Grandfathers — Fiction]*
*I. Levine-Freidus, Gail.   II. Title.*
*PZ7.P948Go      1984      [Fic]      83-15681*
*ISBN 0-02-774950-9*

# Good If It Goes

# Chapter *1*

I came running downcourt on a fast break with Randy trailing me. I stopped at the top of the key and passed to him. He drove under the basket, but Tony Hemingway was all over him, so Randy passed the ball back out to me. I threw up a long set-shot. It was a masterpiece. It had a great arc and a perfect spin, and it went *swish*, right through the basket without even touching the rim. I leaped up into the air. When I landed, I saw Ma's red Subaru.

She was pulling up to the basketball court at three o'clock, just the way she'd promised, not even a minute late. Ma was taking me to see the rabbi so we could all talk about Hebrew school for the coming year. For four years I've been going for Hebrew lessons, ever since I was nine years old, and even though it was only once a week, it seemed as though I was always missing something because of Hebrew school.

This time, my team was practicing basketball after school, for the upcoming Shrimp League season. The

Shrimp League is a basketball league for incredibly short kids, like me and my friend Randy. Randy and I had just started the league, so you can see why I'd want to finish the scrimmage. Anyhow, after my shot went in . . . I always like to leave with a basket . . . I got into Ma's car.

I tossed my books in the back, and I whined a little bit so Ma could tell she was ruining my entire life.

"Sorry, David," Ma said. "We have to go," and she pulled out of the parking lot.

Ma's pretty good at reading my mind, especially when I'm groaning as if I've just been stricken with some awful disease.

After we'd gotten out on the highway, Ma said "Well, I've picked a date."

"For what?" I asked.

"For what?" she said.

"Yeah, Ma, for what?"

"Well, for your bar mitzvah, of course, honey."

"What are you talking about, you picked a date?" I said. "I thought I was supposed to be bar mitzvahed on my birthday, when I turn thirteen." Actually, I was hoping they would all just forget the whole thing.

"Well, first of all, David, you're not *being* bar mitzvahed, you're *having* a bar mitzvah . . . It's a noun, not a verb."

"Come on, Ma. You say "bar mitzvahed" too. I've heard you plenty of times."

"Yes, well, I'm not the one who's having lessons with the rabbi right now. You are."

"Anyhow, am I being . . . *having* my bar mitzvah on my birthday or what?"

"Your birthday happens to fall in the dead of winter, David."

Ma's in local theater and she likes to say things like "the dead of winter."

"Gee, I'm sorry, Ma. Next time I'll get born in July."

"Cute," she said.

Having a bar mitzvah is something you don't have to go through unless you're Jewish, which I am. A bar mitzvah is a ceremony at the temple when a boy, if he's thirteen years old and he's Jewish, is supposed to become a man. It's a lot like a confirmation for a Catholic kid. I'm telling you this because you might not know any Jewish kids. I hardly know any. And I'm Jewish.

"Ma, would you mind telling me what the dead of winter has to do with my bar mitzvah?"

"Well," she said, and she squirmed a little on her pillow. Ma's not exactly what you'd call tall, so she always sits on a pillow when she drives. "We can't have a bar mitzvah in the dead of winter. We need a date when the weather is more reliable."

"Who cares how reliable the weather is?"

"Your Uncle Phil."

"My Uncle Phil?" I said.

"Yes," Ma said. "And my brother. And your grandparents in New York. And the Cashmans and the Waltons and the Wilkenfelds down in North Carolina. They're coming up to see you on your big day."

"Ma," I said, "we are on our way to see a man who thinks Hebrew is the way regular people talk, so I wonder if you'd mind speaking English for now."

"Sorry, David," she said. She reached over and patted my knee. "What I'm trying to say is that if we schedule the bar mitzvah for good weather, then everyone who wants to come can come. But if we schedule it for your birthday, we could have a blizzard or something and a lot of people would not be able to make it."

"Good," I said. "Let's have it when the weather really rots."

"David," Ma said, "have you ever thought of taking this act to Las Vegas? You're really very funny."

Ma squirmed in her seat again. "Honey," she said after a couple of minutes, "you might as well know right now that you will have to go to Hebrew school twice a week now, so that you can learn your haftorah and the *maftir* for your bar mitzvah."

"*Twice a week?*" I screamed. "Are you people out of your minds? What do I have to do this for? Half my life is being stolen away from me."

"Don't you think that's a bit of an overstatement?" she said.

"Hebrew!" I said. "I mean, really! Let's be serious. How many times in the past year have you needed to know Hebrew? Ma, Hebrew just doesn't come up much in real life. Nobody else I know has to do this!"

"That's because there aren't any other Jewish kids in Westbridge," Ma said.

"Oh, yes, there are. There's Eddie Gould."

"He's the only one, then," Ma said.

"Yeah, well Eddie Gould plays shortstop every spring while I'm shlepping off to Hebrew school."

"Some parents send their kids to Hebrew school, and some don't. Like Eddie's parents."

"Yeah, I know. Poor Eddie. Having to play baseball! I wonder how I got so lucky," I said, and I said it in a real ugly way because the idea of Eddie Gould scooping up ground balls while I was off singing "BARUCH ATTO ADONOI" was more than I could stomach.

"David!"

"Ma, I mean it, I don't want to do this thing. I missed baseball last year because of Hebrew school and I don't want to miss basketball this year. I've been practicing. I'm good, Ma, I'm really good and my team's going to be good."

"Honey, I know basketball is important to you. As a matter of fact, I'm extremely proud of you, the way you and Randy set it all up. The Shrimp League is terrific, but . . ."

"Never mind about 'but,'" I said. "I'm in eighth grade this year. We made a rule, Ma. You can't play in the Shrimp League after eighth grade."

"Then you'll play on the high-school team next year."

"Ma, they don't let midgets like me play on high-school basketball teams."

"You'll grow," she said.

"Why should I? You didn't."

"It's different with boys. They grow."

"Oh, really? What's Dad? Chopped liver?" My father is short, too. In fact, you could pile Ma and Dad on top of each other and they probably still wouldn't be as tall as Kareem Abdul-Jabbar.

"Oh, David. You'll grow." Ma was getting annoyed.

"And what if I don't, huh? Did you ever think of that? Look, I *am* going to play basketball this year. And nothing's going to stop me."

My heart was pounding like crazy. I couldn't believe it. It was happening again. Just when I'm going along my merry little way, a stone wall pops up to stop me. Or I fall into a ditch that I didn't see. Why me? I was really upset.

I guess Ma must have been pretty upset, too, because the next thing I knew, a siren was screaming behind us and a cop was signaling Ma over to the side of the road.

"Oh, great! Just what I needed. A ticket," she said, and she slowed down and pulled over and started fumbling around in her pocketbook for her driver's license.

"Ma," I said, "have you ever thought about taking this act to Las Vegas? It's really very funny."

# Chapter 2

So Ma and the rabbi made plans for my bar mitzvah and they didn't talk about things that weren't important, like my opinion, for example. They decided the rabbi would send to the Jewish bookstore in Brookline for my haftorah. That's a section of the Bible that I'd have to chant in Hebrew in front of practically the whole world, and the rabbi would help me learn it. Ma would take care of getting a caterer and a place for the reception and all that other stuff that costs a fortune. And all I had to do was spend about half my life going to Hebrew school. I whined all the way home. Can you blame me?

"Tuesdays and Thursdays?" I kept saying. I was in shock. "Tuesdays and Thursdays?" It was as if I'd just heard that my best friend had been killed in a plane crash and I couldn't believe it. "Tuesdays and Thursdays? Ma, I can't believe you picked Tuesdays and Thursdays!"

"I didn't *pick* Tuesdays and Thurdays," Ma said. "Those are the only days I can take you."

"But Tuesday is the day the Midgets play," I told her. The Westbridge Midgets are my Shrimp League team, and Randy and I had spent two days phoning every kid in the league so we could come up with the perfect day of the week when every kid could play.

"The rabbi doesn't teach classes on Wednesday and Friday," Ma replied. "The rabbi is a very busy man."

"Then what about Monday? I could go on Mondays and Thursdays."

"David, you know on Mondays I have to take Markie to the conservatory."

Markie is my little brother. He goes to Hebrew school, too. He's ten and he's supposed to be some kind of musical genius, which is why he gets to go to the music conservatory every Monday.

"Let him drop out," I said. "Going to the conservatory is dumb, anyhow."

"David!"

My mother has about eighty-four different ways of saying "David," and this particular one meant, "David, stop being mean to your little brother."

So then I brooded for a little while and Ma kept driving and not saying anything. After a minute or so I said, "Tuesdays and Thursdays? Ma, I can't believe you picked Tuesdays and Thursdays," and we started all over again.

At dinner that night Ma tried to talk to Dad about the plans she and the rabbi had made for my bar mitzvah. But Markie kept hogging the conversation, which is something he has a habit of doing at dinner while normal people are eating. Unfortunately, Markie had seen a music synthesizer that day and he carried on as if he found a cure for cancer or something.

"Dad, this thing is incredible," he said. "It's got four VCO's and three keyboard assign modes. It's got a five octave keyboard."

Markie went on like that for a while. He might as well have been talking in Turkish for all the sense he made. But Dad's really interested in that kind of stuff, and he was nodding his head and saying, "Hey, that's great, Markie," just as if Markie was making sense. Personally, I was getting sick with synthersizeritis.

"Some day, so help me, I'm going to have one of those," Markie said.

"Maybe you will," Dad said, "maybe you will. If I keep getting good reports on your piano lessons."

"Andy Calamari's father bought him one," Markie said. "He's loaded."

"Yeah, well, *your* father isn't," I said, figuring it was my chance to grab the conversation. "And speaking of money, Dad," I said, "I've been thinking that a bar mitzvah party runs into a lot of money, and you don't have to . . ."

"Well, Markie, they make smaller synthesizers, too," Dad said, "and maybe you'd better be thinking about that," and as he and Markie went on and on about synthesizers it was pretty obvious to everybody that I didn't exist and was only imagining that I did.

Finally Ma put up her hands, gave Markie a real stern look and said, "*Eat*." That's when she finally got a chance to tell Dad that she and the rabbi had decided that April 21st would be a great day for me to be bar mitzvahed. I

9

decided we weren't finished discussing the matter, especially since it was clear my father had no idea that my life was about to be ruined. He just said, "Fine, fine" and then he started wondering out loud where he could get the best deal on a synthesizer.

Around eight o'clock it seemed like a good time to reopen the bar mitzvah discussion. Ma and Dad were both in the family room. Dad was stretched out on the couch watching a fight on television. A couple of middle-weights were beating each other's heads in. Ma was sitting in her easy chair reading a novel about some artist who got fed up with everything and took a hike to Tahiti. And Markie was in the living room banging away on the piano as if it had done some terrible thing to him.

I strolled over to a spot in the family room about half-way between Ma and Dad and I stood there as if I was waiting for a tip. I figured my own parents would notice me. They didn't. I cleared my throat. No response. I folded my arms. Silence. I sighed. Nothing. I tapped my foot. More nothing. I tapped it louder. Still nothing.

"Yoo-hoo," I finally said. "It's me, your son, David. Remember me?"

Ma looked up. Dad didn't.

"David," my father said, "will you move out of the way, please. You're distracting me."

I moved about an inch.

"Hey, come on," he said. "*Move.*"

I moved completely out of the way. Fast.

"I want to talk to you guys about something," I said.

"Later," Dad grumbled.

"Now feels like an excellent time," I said.

"*Later*," Dad said.

Ma knew what I wanted to talk about so she told Dad it was something we should discuss right away. Then she got up and turned off the television. Dad looked at her as if this proved there was a world-wide plot to get him. He sat up on the couch. "Okay, okay," he said, "what's up?"

I took a deep breath. "I don't want to go to Hebrew school this year," I said.

There was a very long pause. Then my father said, "So, David, I hear you don't want to go to Hebrew school anymore. Is that right?"

"Yes, sir."

"Well, guess what? I don't want to go to work tomorrow, either. Did you know that? But I'm going to work. I'm going to do what I have to do. And so are you. Do I make myself clear?"

"I'm not going," I said. "I missed baseball because of Hebrew school. I missed soccer because of Hebrew school. This is my last chance to play on a basketball team. You guys have got to see how important this is."

"You're being ridiculous," my father said.

"Why? Because I'd rather play basketball than learn some language that's written backwards?"

"David, it's not written backwards," my mother said. "Just right to left instead of left to right."

"It's backwards!" I said. "It starts at the end, doesn't it, and it ends at the beginning."

"The pages just go in a different way."

"Well, it's dumb," I said. "I bet you and Dad can't even remember how to read Hebrew."

"We're not talking about us," my father said. "We're

11

talking about you. And the answer is no. You can't drop out of Hebrew school."

"No?"

"That's what I said, David." Dad was standing now. "*No*."

"Look, honey," my mother said, "I know it isn't easy for you to have to go off to Fitchburg every week and take Hebrew lessons far away from your friends." She looked at Dad. He was frowning. "It was easier for your father and me when we were kids. There were more Jewish kids in the cities where we lived. We could be with our friends and still learn Hebrew. It's different for you, but . . ."

"But you're going to do it just like we did," Dad said, "whether you like it or not."

"But . . ."

"But nothing," Dad barked.

"Why?"

"Because you are our son and you are Jewish and you are going to be thirteen and you are going to keep the tradition. You will go to Hebrew school twice a week and you will learn your haftorah. You will not break the chain just because you want to. A bar mitzvah is all about becoming a man, David, and being a man means you don't get to do everything you want to do."

"Oh," I said. "I thought being a man meant you had some control over your own life."

"Don't give me any wise remarks, David. You will do what you're told. It's that simple. No discussion."

When Dad says, "no discussion," what he means is *No Discussion*. Ma and I looked at each other and I stomped out of the room.

12

# Chapter 3

On the way to science class the next day I grabbed Randy
in the hallway and I told him there was this very slight
chance that I might be going to Hebrew school twice a
week and that maybe I'd end up missing a couple of
Shrimp League games and a few practices. Randy looked
at me as if I was crazy. "I must have heard you wrong," he
said, "tell me again at lunch."

Randy sat beside me in the cafeteria and I told him
again.

Randy always takes my side, which is what a good
friend does, and after I told him what was going on, he
said that Ma and Dad and the rabbi and the Wilkenfelds
and the Cashmans and almost everybody else was nuts
and that anybody who thought a bar mitzvah was more
important than basketball should be put in a home somewhere until they found their brains.

"When are you supposed to start?" he said.

"Next week."

"You know, we're not going to win a game if you don't

play," Randy said, which made me feel great and lousy at the same time, if you know what I mean.

"So help me out," I said. "Think of a way I can get out of this mess."

"What about your grandfather?"

"Max?"

"Yeah, Max. He'll help you. He always helps you."

Randy was right. If there was one guy I could always turn to for help it was Max Levene. Grampa! Practically the best friend I ever had. "Yeah," I said, "he always helps me out, but . . ."

"Well, he can convince your parents that basketball is more important than Hebrew school. They'll listen to him because he's old."

"Yeah, and he's smart too," I said. I was getting excited. "Yeah, Max will help me. He doesn't even believe in God. Why would he care about a bar mitzvah? You're a genius, Randy!"

I was so happy that I gave him my chocolate pudding.

When I got home from school I went straight to the phone and dialed Max Levene's number.

Max's phone rang for a long time. Finally, Nana answered. Nana's my grandmother, but everybody calls her Nana.

"Hello?"

"Hi, Nana, how you doing?" I said. "It's me, David."

"Well, well, David. To what do I owe such an honor, this phone call?"

"Oh, I just wanted to say hello. And, you know, to see how you and Grampa are doing. Is Grampa there? Can I talk to him?"

"Your grandfather's here, darling, but he's taking a little nap. He's been tired lately, so it's good he gets a rest, don't you think?"

"Oh, sure," I said. I knew Grampa had been tired a lot since his heart attack.

Then Nana told me what she was cooking. Nana is always cooking. I made her promise to have Grampa call me as soon as he got up. After I hung up I felt a lot better.

I tried to do my science homework while I waited for Max to call. It was all about convection cells, whatever they are. But my mind kept drifting. Good old Max, I thought. He was always calling me up and he'd say, "Hello, David? It's me, Max Levene. Your grandfather." Really. I mean who else could it be? But that's the way he'd call every time.

I was just starting to make some sense out of the convection cells when the phone rang.

"Hello?"

"Hello, David?"

"Yes." Here it comes, I thought.

"This is Max Levene, your grandfather."

"Who?" I said. "Max who?"

"Max Levene. Your grandfather."

"Levene," I said. "Levene? It does sound familiar."

"It's me," he said, "Max Levene."

"Oh, Grampa, it's you huh? I hear you been sleeping on the job. What gives?"

"Gives? What is 'gives'? I'm an old man, a busy old man. I need sometimes a nap."

"Yeah? So what did you make today, Grampa?"

Grampa was always making something. He used to

have a tailor shop, so mostly he makes slip covers and stuff like that now, but he can do pretty much anything he wants with his hands. Ma says Markie and I inherited Grampa's great hands, which is why I can shoot a basket from thirty feet and Markie can play the piano like Stevie Wonder.

"Today, David, I finished up a little shelf which I put into the hole in the wall."

"What hole in the wall?"

"The hole behind the picture. Above the sofa. You remember, David? Where there used to be the safe."

"Oh, yeah," I said. The safe. I remembered how excited I was when I was a kid and Grampa pulled away the picture and showed me the safe. He was always coming up with surprises like that. And for years he had let me keep things in his safe, my "Top Secret" stuff I called it. It wasn't until he mentioned it now that I realized I wasn't keeping things in his safe anymore.

"Well," Grampa said, "I took out the safe, and I put in, instead, a shelf."

"Why?"

"Because this way your grandmother can put on the shelf all the things she needs for when she sits on the sofa and sews. She can reach up and get a needle or thread or a thimble. She should have whatever she needs, just like that. It should be handy. It's a very practical thing, this shelf."

"Right, Grampa," I said. "Good for you. So, look Grampa . . ."

"What is it, David, something is troubling you?"

"Well, sort of."

"Are you okay, my grandson?"

"Oh, I'm great. It's just that, you know, things could be better."

"Oh? What is this?"

"I can't tell you, Grampa, not over the phone. I have to talk in person."

"Well, good. Then tomorrow we talk, huh?"

"Tomorrow?"

"Yes," he said. "Tomorrow is Rosh Hashanah. You will be here, your mother and your father and my other grandson. You know who I mean, the musician?"

"Markie."

"Yes, Markie," he said. "The little *shmendrick.*" Shmendrick is a Yiddish word for a little kid. Max uses a lot of Yiddish words. "You will all be here for dinner, then we talk."

"Oh, yeah," I said. "I forgot."

"You forgot Rosh Hashanah?"

"Well, you know how it is, Grampa, you get busy."

"Hmmn," he said.

"But, look, Grampa," I said, "we can't talk at dinner. It's kind of private, you know. Just you and me. Man to man."

"I see," he said. And then after a while he said, "David, you don't want to eat this dinner when you have a troubled mind. Nana's been cooking this meal I think for a week. So I tell you what, my grandson, we will go to temple, and then you and me, we go for a walk and we will talk, like you say, man to man. But, David, listen to me, in the meanwhile you should do me a favor. I like to solve a good mystery, so, David, before you leave the phone, I need a clue."

"A clue?"

"To what is troubling a boy who is twelve years old."

"A clue, huh? Well . . . it has to do with basketball."

"Basketball? From me you expect talk about basketball? Ha, it seems to me you got the wrong boy, David, the wrong boy."

"I don't think so, Grampa."

"Hmmn. Okay, David, I'll see you tomorrow for Nana's chicken soup and for talking in person. Good night."

"Good night, Max Levene," I said. "This is your grandson, David, signing off."

"Basketball yet!" he said, and he hung up.

# Chapter 4

The trip to Newton, which is where Grampa and Nana live, was weird. I was thinking most of the time and hardly noticed that we were driving for an hour. Ma and Dad were playing alphabet games . . . that's what we do when we're all in the car . . . and Markie spent the whole trip playing his flutophone. Markie plays about ninety-two instruments and he and the other kids have their own band. They call themselves "Popcorn." Markie is kind of mentally ill about music. Anyhow, I didn't do too well on the alphabet games, where you try to find something on the highway that begins with the letter *A* then *B* and so forth, because all the time I was trying to concentrate on what I would say to Max Levene to get him on my side against this bunch of weirdos who were going to cheat me out of my one chance to play on a basketball team.

After we got there we went to Grampa and Nana's temple in Newton, the way we do every year. That's what you do on Rosh Hashanah, you go to temple and then you eat a big dinner. Rosh Hashanah is the Jewish New Year, and to get into temple that day you've got to have reserved seats. The rest of the year, it's like the Boston Celtics are playing the Cleveland Cavaliers or somebody and there's plenty of seats. But on the holidays it's like the Celtics are playing the Philadelphia 76ers, with Julius Erving and Moses Malone, and if you don't have your tickets ahead of time you can forget about going. But Grampa and Nana reserved us all seats.

Going to temple was okay. At least Markie couldn't play his flutophone there, and it gave me some more time to think about what I would say to Max.

When we got back to my grandparents' house late in the afternoon, Max told everybody else to go on inside.

"I take David for a walk," he said.

Grampa led me down behind his house into some woods that stretch for about a mile, I guess, all the way to the turnpike. In the autumn here the leaves on the trees are gold and red and lots of other colors and on a sunny afternoon like this was, they're just incredibly bright. It was real basketball weather.

"To the stream," Grampa said. There's a stream down behind Grampa's house, which is the main reason he bought the house years ago. He lived near a stream when he was a kid in Germany.

"You know," Max Levene said as we moved down the hill kind of slowly because Max isn't all that young anymore, "when I was a boy in Germany my father would walk with me and my brothers and sisters down to the

20

stream on the first day of Rosh Hashanah. There we would say a prayer and then we would shake out our pockets in the stream. It was said that we were shaking away our sins. This is a custom called *Tashlich*. Then we would walk home and Mama would be waiting with home-baked challa and wine and we would dip the challa in honey and everyone would wish everyone a sweet new year."

When we got down by the stream, Grampa reached in his pockets and took out his handkerchief and his keys and put them on the ground by a tree. Then he stood by the stream and he yanked his pockets inside out and he shook them over the stream. "David," he said, "you got some sins you want to get rid of?"

"I guess," I said, and I stood next to him and shook out my pockets, though I felt a little silly doing it.

We sat for a while by the stream without talking and then Max Levene said, "What is the problem?"

"Grampa," I said, "I've got to play basketball this year. This is absolutely my last chance. I'll never make the team next year in high school. I'm too short. Randy and I started the Shrimp League just so kids like us could play on a team."

"So why is this a problem?"

"Ma and Dad won't let me play," I said.

"Hmmn," Grampa said. He says "hmmn" a lot. "This is strange," he said. "Your mother and your father love you. Why would they not let you do something that is so important to you? They must have a very good reason."

"No, Grampa, they don't have any good reason."

"Oh? So what is this reason they have that is not so good?"

"Hebrew school."

"Hebrew school? This is a problem?"

"My bar mitzvah!" I said. "I'm getting my haftorah pretty soon and that means I have to go to Hebrew school twice a week to learn it. Tuesdays and Thursdays! And the Shrimp League games are on Tuesdays, and even if they weren't, there just wouldn't be time for everything, with homework and all."

"Hmmn," my grandfather said.

"It's just not fair, Grampa. I don't care about being bar mitzvahed. It's not important to anybody except them, but they won't listen to me. You're the only one who can convince them. They'll listen to you."

Grampa didn't say anything for a long time. He just stared at the stream. Then he said, "What makes you think that I would tell your parents you should not go to Hebrew school, my grandson?"

"Because you're an atheist," I said. "You don't believe in God."

"Agnostic," he said.

"'Agnostic'? What's that?"

"It means I'm not sure about God."

"Well, if you're not so sure there's a God then you don't believe in bar mitzvahs, right?"

"My grandson," he said, "it is sometimes difficult for me to believe there is a God who should allow what has happened to my family and our people over the years. You know what I'm talking?"

22

"You mean about the Nazis and the concentration camps and all that?"

"Yes, David," he said. "All that." He said it more to himself than to me. Most of Max Levene's family had been killed in Germany because they were Jewish. "So," Grampa said, "this is not a God I can believe in, though I don't say you shouldn't. This you must decide for yourself. But I believe in our people, David, and it seems to me that if there is a God he would want you to be a bar mitzvah boy like your father before you. It is the tradition."

"I know, I know," I said. There was that word again. *Tradition*. "But, Grampa," I said, "I don't believe in tradition."

"Oh?"

"Yeah, Grampa, really! I thought about it, I really did, and I think that what's going on now is what's really important, not a bunch of stuff that happened years ago."

"So you do not believe in tradition? Of this you are sure?"

"Yes," I said. "I'm sure."

"Oh," Grampa said, "I am so relieved. The money I will save."

"What are you talking about, the money you'll save?" I said. For a minute I thought Max Levene was getting nutty.

"On your birthday presents," he said. "And on Chanukah I'll save a fortune. Yes, yes. With all the money I'll save, I'll buy maybe a new car."

"Grampa, what have birthday presents got to do with it? And Chanukah presents?"

"It is tradition," he said. "Nothing more. Why do we give a present to a boy on his birthday? Because it is the tradition, that's why. And Chanukah. Tell me, David, your Christian friends, do they also think tradition is not important? Their parents will be happy to know this. No more Christmas shopping!"

"But that's different," I said. "Birthday presents and Christmas presents, that's not the same as being bar mitzvahed."

"I know," he said. "Being a bar mitzvah boy is even more important."

For a while we didn't say anything. We sat by the stream. I kept picking up twigs and breaking them in half, as if that would do any good. And Grampa just looked kind of peaceful the way he does when he's thinking.

Finally, Grampa spoke.

He lifted his hand a little bit and he said, "You see the stream, David. The traditions are like a stream, too, a stream that flows through the generations of Jewish people. You don't do this bar mitzvah for God, my grandson, you do it for your people in the past and in the future. It is the tradition, and the Hebrew language of your haftorah is the tradition also and that is what makes the Jewish people who they are. If there's no tradition, there's no people."

"Eddie Gould is not getting bar mitzvahed," I said. It was a pretty stupid thing to think of but I didn't know what else to say.

"Then that is why you should," Grampa said.

"Huh?"

"When a boy does not have his bar mitzvah or when we do not light the candles on Chanukah or we do not eat the matzo at Passover, it is like throwing a twig into the stream. One twig, David, will not hurt your people. It will float away. Like our sins. But if you throw a twig and I throw a twig and Eddie Gould throws a twig, and everybody throws a twig, do you know what will happen?"

"The stream will stop," I said.

"Right, my grandson," Max Levene said. He reached over and patted my knee and smiled at me. "If there is a God, he does not want his streams to stop. He would want you to have your bar mitzvah."

"But what if there isn't a God?" I said.

"If there is not a God, then you must certainly have your bar mitzvah."

"Why?"

"Because if there is not a God, we need all the help we can get to keep our people together."

"What about helping me?" I said. "I need help, too, you know. Basketball is important."

"I will help you," my grandfather said. "I will help you with some advice. Find a way. You are a bright boy and if you really want to play basketball you will find a way to do this and to help your people stay together also." Then he added, "Sholem aleichem."

"'Sholem aleichem'?" I said. "What does that mean?"

"It means 'peace unto you,'" he said. "Now you say to me 'aleichem sholem.'"

"What does that mean?"

"It means 'and unto you peace, also.'"

25

"Aleichem sholem," I said.

I felt pretty lousy as we walked back up through the woods and into the house. Everyone was standing around the kitchen when we walked in. Ma looked at me as if the answer to some question were written on my face. Then she looked at Max. Then Dad looked at me. Then he looked at Max. Nobody said anything for a minute. Then Nana said, "Come, everybody come into the dining room."

Nana had baked a beautiful challa and it was sitting on the dining room table. It's a big loaf of bread shaped like a crown, which Jewish people eat on special holidays. We all gathered around the table while Grampa sliced the challa. Then we each took a piece. Nana walked around carrying a bowl of honey. We dipped our bread in the honey and everybody wished everybody else a sweet new year. Dad came over and put his arm around me.

"So did you have a nice walk with your grandfather?" he said.

"I've had better," I said.

Dad squeezed me a little tighter. Grampa poured the wine, and when everybody had a glass, Dad lifted his high in the air. "To David," he said, "to David."

# *Chapter 5*

So, of course, I ended up shlepping off to Hebrew school twice a week. On Thursdays Ma would drive Markie and me to the temple the way she always had, and after I finished my lesson I'd do some homework while Markie had his lesson. And on Tuesdays Ma would take just me, so the rabbi could help me study and learn my haftorah for my bar mitzvah.

The Shrimp League got started without me, but I was kind of proud of it, anyhow, because the schedule went just the way Randy and I planned. We had six teams: the Marlboro Dwarfs, the Northboro Guppies, the Lancaster Gnats, the Sterling Elves, and the Bolton Bumblebees. And, of course, the Westbridge Midgets. That's the team I was on, except that I couldn't play in regular games because of Hebrew school. We didn't have uniforms or anything like that, but we had plenty of kids who had volunteered to be timekeepers and keep statistics, and we even had some fans . . . girls who liked short kids, and the mothers who drove the teams to the basketball courts.

Anyhow, between Hebrew school and regular school and science homework and math homework and studying for my bar mitzvah and going to Shrimp League practices, you would have needed a shoehorn to squeeze anything else into my life. And then, of all the things in the world to happen, I met a girl.

The funny thing is that the night I fell in love was the night I had decided to shave my head, and if I hadn't met Kelly O'Neil I'd probably be bald right now. About a month after school started we had our first eighth-grade dance, and before the dance I stood in front of my mirror for a long time trying to decide whether I could shave it with my Dad's electric razor, or if I'd need a lawn mower.

I'm always disappointed when I look in the mirror. The main reason is that my reflection is so low. But the other thing is that I've always hated my hair. I've got a mop just like Ma's, except that hers is on the end of a stick and mine is on my head and has more curls than a French poodle. On the night of the dance my curls seemed especially tight and I was afraid that if I did get the courage to ask a girl to dance, one of my curls might uncoil and smack her in the eye and she'd sue me.

By the time my father dropped me off at the dance I had decided to play it safe. I wouldn't dance with anybody. I was in charge of refreshments for the first hour, anyway.

Even before I got my cash box set up, there was a line of girls waiting for Cokes and stuff. Jennie Tabat was first in line and she wanted a soda and a brownie. I had worked the refreshment stand before and I have to admit I'm practically a genius at it. So I brilliantly poured her soda into a paper cup and snatched a brownie out of the card-board holder and made change and tossed the empty can into the barrel, and by the time I had waited on three or four girls I was really in the groove. I had my routine down pat. But then all of a sudden there was Kelly O'Neil standing in front of me, except I didn't know that was her name. She was beautiful. And she had long brown hair. And big brown eyes. And an incredible smile. And, wonder of wonders . . . she was short.

"What's your pleasure, lady?" I said. I tried to sound real cool but my voice sounded as if someone were stepping on my foot. "Pretzels? Potato chips? We've got a full-service operation here."

"I'd like an orange soda, David," she said. She knew my name. She sounded like an angel.

So I looked over at the soda chest and I called, "Hey, Bub, one orange soda for the lady." Then I jumped over to the soda chest. "Coming right up," I called back to the counter. Then I reached in and tried to snatch up a can of soda and I splashed icy water all over my sleeve. Then I rushed back to the counter, dripping water on the floor, and I opened the can and started pouring it for her. "He's a little slow," I said, "new on the job, you know how it is." But while I was doing this routine my hand was shaking and after I filled Kelly's cup I knocked it over and the orange soda spilled all over the counter and dripped on Kelly's shoes.

"Ohmigosh, I'm sorry!" I said. I felt like my face was on fire. It was the second worst moment in my entire life. The first worst moment came right after, when I dashed back to the soda chest to get her another orange soda and I slipped on the icy water and went flying to the floor, idiotically shouting "Hey, Bub, another soda for the lady."

By this time a dozen kids had gathered by the refreshment counter so they could watch me make a fool of myself. You could have fried a pound of bacon on my face, but I had to laugh along with them. What choice did I have? I crawled back to the counter with another can of orange soda, which I didn't dare open. I put it down on the counter next to a paper cup and I said, "Here you are. It's on the house. Come back later and I'll show you some more tricks."

"Sure, David," Kelly said. She smiled at me. Then she led the other kids away from the counter. I stood there with a wet sleeve and a red face and I tried to figure out which would be the best way for me to get out of town fast. I guess the only reason I didn't hitchhike to South Dakota or something was that I wanted to see Kelly again.

By the time my hour behind the counter was up, Kelly hadn't come back, and I had decided I'd find her and explain that I wasn't always an idiot and then I'd ask her to dance and then maybe later on I'd ask her to marry me. For a long time I just watched her from the other side of the gym. My heart was pounding like a basketball on a fast break. She was shorter than me! I couldn't get over it. She was standing with some other girls, talking and laughing and just generally being short.

The first time I got the courage to go near her I circled around the gym and I came within ten feet of her. But my mouth was so dry you would have thought I'd crossed the Sahara Desert. I decided to go back to the refreshment counter and get a soda. I saw Kelly and Emily Matson look over at me. Were they talking about me, I wondered. After I gulped down my soda I started working my way around again. This time I got so I was only about three feet away. Right about then I was feeling a little hungry and I thought I'd better go back and get a brownie before I talked to Kelly. But on the way back I ran into Randy and I told him what was going on and he told me not to be such a spineless, gutless, chicken-hearted, cowardly little weasel. So I went back, and when I got near Kelly I started looking around to see where Randy was so I could sneak back to the refreshment counter without him seeing me. And while I was gawking around trying to find Randy, I bumped into a girl. It was Kelly.

"Oh, sorry," I said. "Pretty dumb."

"Un-huh," she said.

"Actually I've been meaning to talk to you sometime, anyhow," I said, "so this is a good chance." I sounded like a businessman, and I was beginning to wish I had skipped town. "I just wanted to tell you that I'm not always a jerk."

"Oh, I know that," she said. I was hoping she'd say more but she didn't.

Finally I knew I had to go away or say something, so I said, "You must be new in Westbridge."

"Twelve years," she said.

"Huh?"

"Twelve years," she said again. "I was born here."

"Oh," I said. "I never saw you before."

"I went to Girl's Catholic school," she said. "This is my first year here."

"Why did you change schools?"

"Boys," she said.

"What's your name?" I said.

"My name?" She smiled "First, what's your name?"

"I thought you knew my name was David," I said.

"I do. But I bet you have a last name, too."

"Oh! Newman."

"David O'Newman, that's funny."

"Sure it's funny," I said. "But that's not my name. It's just David Newman, not 'David O'Newman.'"

She smiled and put out her hand for me to shake. "My name's Kelly O'Neil," she said, "Only it's Kelly O'Neil, not 'Kelly Oh. Neil.'"

Then when I couldn't think of anything brilliant to say she looked into my eyes and said, "Were you going to ask me to dance?"

"Oh," I said, "you probably wouldn't want to dance with me, I mean after I spilled soda on you and everything."

"You never know until you ask," she said. And just then Jimmy Evans came along and took her hand and said, "Let's dance, Kelly. It's the last one," and she looked at me and I didn't know what to say, so she said, "Okay," to Jimmy. I should have hated his guts right then, but actually Jimmy's a pretty nice kid.

But before she walked off with Jimmy Evans, Kelly smiled at me and she said, "See you, David."

"See you," I said.

"And, David," she said.

"Yeah?"

"I like your curls."

After the dance Ma was waiting to drive me home in her Subaru.

32

"How was the dance?" she said.

"It was good," I said. I was floating and kind of dazed. "I met a girl."

"Oh?"

"Her name's Kelly."

"Did you dance with her?"

"No," I said. "But she loves my mop and she's not going to sue me."

"Sounds like a nice girl," Ma said.

# Chapter 6

I guess everybody gets lucky once in a while. Even me.
My lucky day came ten days after the dance. I know it
was exactly ten days because I had circled the date of the
dance on my calendar and printed in a big *K* for Kelly. I
hadn't talked to Kelly but I had thought about her a lot. It
was as if somebody had shoved a giant tape cassette in my
head and all it did was play thoughts about Kelly all day.
I thought about her even when I was thinking about convection cells, basketball and Hebrew school. Then one
day God must have taken pity on me because I got to skip
Hebrew school, talk to Kelly and play basketball. All on
the same day.

I was standing outside school one Tuesday waiting for
Ma to pick me up and drive me to Hebrew class, when the
school secretary came running out and said, "Your mother
called. She said to take the bus home, the rabbi canceled
classes for today."

I was free. On a Tuesday. I couldn't believe it. I could
go home and change my clothes and actually play in the

Shrimp League game against the Northboro Guppies. When I got on the bus I practically danced to the back of it where there were some empty seats and when I got about halfway down the bus I heard, "Hi, David!"

It was Kelly, sitting next to Jennifer Pratt. On *my* bus. I couldn't believe it. I said, "Hi, Kelly!" which I guess is a perfectly normal thing to say, but somehow it still sounded goofy. Then I kept walking to the back because I knew the bus driver would yell at me if I stopped to talk. Besides, I didn't know what to say.

So I sat near the back of the bus practically drilling a hole into the back of Kelly's head with my eyes. I was trying to send her mental messages. It must have worked, because the next time the bus stopped, Kelly got up and came to the back of the bus and sat down in the seat next to me on the other side of the aisle.

"So, how you been, David Oh Newman?" she asked.

"Oh, I've been great," I said. "How come you're on this bus?" I noticed that I wasn't as nervous when I was actually talking to Kelly as I was when I was just thinking about talking to her.

"I'm going home with Jennifer Pratt. I'm going to have supper at her house."

"Oh."

"Do you know Jennifer?" Kelly asked.

"Oh, sure," I said, "I know everybody," and I kind of waved my hand out, being very cool, except that I smacked into the books on my lap and they went flying onto the floor and my papers spilled all over the place.

"Oh, David, I'll help you," Kelly said and she leaned over and handed me my science book, and then we started picking up papers, with our heads actually touching. But then Kelly said, "David, what's this?" She was holding my Hebrew book. I could feel my face go red.

"It's nothing," I said.

"What do you mean, nothing?" She was flipping through the pages. "Come on, David, what is it?"

"Hebrew," I said.

"Hebrew? Really?" she said. She sounded excited. "It looks like Chinese, all those funny little lines."

"I go to Hebrew school," I said. "Twice a week," I added, figuring I'd get a little sympathy.

"Oh, you're lucky!" Kelly said.

"Lucky?"

"Sure. I always thought it would be great to learn a foreign language. I'm taking French this year. But Hebrew? You're probably the only kid in Westbridge who speaks Hebrew. Say something in Hebrew."

"*Ah Nee O Hayv O's Och*," I blurted out like an idiot.

That means I love you and that's how it would look if it were written out in English letters instead of Hebrew letters. I couldn't believe I had said it. I was sure glad that Kelly didn't speak Hebrew.

She smiled. "That sounds nice," she said. "What does it mean?"

"Huh?"

"What does it mean?"

"Oh, nothing," I said. "It's just some words."

"Oh, really, David?" she said. "The Hebrews have words that don't mean anything?"

"You wouldn't believe I forgot what they mean, would you?"

36

"No," she said. "Come on, David Oh Newman, what does it mean?"

"It means 'I like you,'" I said.

"Oh," Kelly said. Then we both got quiet for a minute and we both pretended we were looking out the windows of the bus. Then Kelly said, "What's this little booklet?"

"It's my haftorah," I said. She was holding it in her hands and turning it upside down as if she could figure out how to read it.

"What's that?"

"It's just something I have to study," I said. "I'm going to be thirteen pretty soon and I'm going to have a bar mitzvah. It's kind of dumb but my parents want me to do it. That's why I have to go to Hebrew school twice a week. When you get bar mitzvahed there's a lot of stuff you have to learn, blessings and things. But the big thing is the haftorah."

"Well, what is it?"

"It's hard to explain," I said. "First I'd have to explain what the Torah is." I figured Kelly would be really bored by all this Jewish stuff.

"We've got time," she said. Then she turned sideways so she was facing me and she put her elbows on her knees and she put her face on her hands and looked up at me with those incredible brown eyes that made me melt and she said, "So what's a Torah?"

"It's the first five books of the Bible," I said. Only they're written in Hebrew on this huge scroll. Every temple has one. Every week the rabbi reads a section from the Torah, then the next week he'll read the next section and

37

so forth for about a year until he gets to the end and then he'll go back to the beginning and start over."

"So a half Torah is half of that?" Kelly said.

"Huh? No, not 'half Torah.' It's *haftorah*," I said and I spelled it out for her. "It's a section from a different part of the Bible. It's from the Prophets and it always has something to do with the section of the Torah that's being read that day by the rabbi. The rabbi's got a book where he can look up any day and find out what section of the Torah he'll be reading, and then if somebody's going to be bar mitzvahed that day he orders a booklet that has the right haftorah in it, so the bar mitzvah boy can study. The rabbi gets all his books at a Jewish book store in Brookline. This one is for April 21st, which is when I'm going to be bar mitzvahed and I've got to spend practically my whole life learning it for the next six months."

Kelly looked like she was really interested in what I was saying. But she looked confused, too.

"But if you can read Hebrew, why don't you just read it?"

"Well, for one thing I don't read Hebrew all that great." I said. "I've only been going to Hebrew school once a week until this fall, and it takes a long time to really learn it. But that's not all. You don't just read your haftorah. You chant it."

"Chant it?"

"Yeah, see these funny little lines above and below the letters?" I leaned over and pointed to the little accent marks, and I made sure my head accidentally touched hers and my fingers just happened to brush against Kelly's hands. "They're called *trope*. They're like musical notes and I have to learn every single one. You don't learn to chant in regular Hebrew school."

"Oh, David," she said, as if she'd just heard I was dying and she was really sorry about it. "You mean you have to learn how to read a foreign language and you have to learn to read music, too?"

"Something like that," I said. I showed her how Hebrew goes from right to left and from the back of the book to the front. I showed her real slowly so I could stay close to her for a while, and I could smell her hair.

"Who teaches you all of this?" Kelly asked.

"The rabbi," I said. "Do you know what a rabbi is?"

"Sure. He's like a priest, right, but for a temple instead of a church. Or is it called a synagogue?"

I was surprised that she knew the word *synagogue*. "You can call it either one," I said. "Old people call it a shul. It doesn't matter. Anyhow, my mother takes me to Temple Beth-El. That's in Fitchburg."

"Fitchburg? Isn't there someplace closer?"

"No. There aren't many Jewish families in Westbridge, so there's no temple."

"Too bad," she said. She touched my arm. I couldn't believe it.

"It's not so bad, really," I said. "It's a nice little synagogue, and Ma says it reminds her a lot of the one she went to when she was a kid. See, my rabbi teaches the Ashkenazic pronunciation of Hebrew, and that's what my parents learned when they went to Hebrew school. There's another pronunciation called Sephardic, and that's what most synagogues have switched to."

"Why?" Kelly asked.

"I don't know, really. I guess because that's what is spoken in Israel. My parents probably like the Fitchburg synagogue so much because it's so old-fashioned. Anyhow, while I'm having my lesson, my mother goes shopping and then we usually go out for something to eat. There's this great pizza place in Fitchburg."

I wanted to say, "We could go there sometime," but I didn't have the guts.

"Ohmigosh, there's my stop," I said. I glanced out the window and saw that I was home. "See you," I said, and I got out of my seat wondering if Kelly liked me or if she was just interested in Hebrew for some strange reason.

"See you," she said, and when I was halfway to the front of the bus she called, "David!"

I turned around.

"Your haftorah," she said, and she waved it at me. And when I stumbled back to take it out of her hand and thank her she smiled and said, "You know, I'd really love to go to a temple or a synagogue or a shul sometime."

"You would?" I said. "Yeah. Sure. Maybe. Sure. See you. Bye," and a lot of other really brilliant things like that. By the time I got off the bus I was smiling so hard I thought my face would crack.

After I got home and put my sneakers on, I called Randy and then his mother picked me up and drove the Midgets over to Northboro and I played in one of the greatest basketball games in the history of the world. We beat the Guppies by ten points, but actually they played pretty good and it was really close until the last five minutes.

And I was the star. That's not just my opinion. Everybody said so. So I have to admit it. I was great. I scored sixteen points, most of them on long bombs from the outside. But I didn't hog the ball or anything. I picked up a lot of assists, feeding Randy on fast breaks, and Phil Clinton, who's got a great hook shot but usually never gets to use it in a game because the taller kids block it. I even got a whole mess of rebounds, which I never would have gotten playing against tall kids.

After the game all the kids said I played good enough to make the school team even if I was short. And I started thinking maybe they were right, maybe I could make the school team. But I knew that even if I did I wouldn't be able to play, because I'd be going to Hebrew school until April. Then I started getting mad at Hebrew school again and I decided I'd go on strike.

But it was hard to stay mad because every time I thought about Hebrew school it reminded me of Kelly and how interested she was in my haftorah and all that stuff and when I thought about Kelly it made me happy and I forgot about everything and just thought about her.

# Chapter 7

It seemed as if every time I looked at my mother for the
rest of that week she was sitting at the dining room table,
making lists. That's how you plan a bar mitzvah, you
make lists, lots of lists. Ma was really getting into this bar
mitzvah thing, which Dad seemed glad about; she was
like a general planning a war. There was the Things-to-
Arrange-For list, with items like: The Band, The Caterers
and The Reception Hall, and there was the Definitely-
Invite list, and the Maybe-Invite list and the Food list.
And of course there was the Hotels list, which Ma and I
took with us on Saturday when we went to check out
hotels for the bar mitzvah.

After a bar mitzvah there's usually a big reception like a
wedding reception and you have to have a hotel to hold it
in, and you've got to plan way in advance.

At each hotel we went to, Ma made a list of good points
and bad points. They were all fine with me as long as they
had a dance floor. There would be a band at the reception
and all I cared about was dancing with Kelly.

Three of the places Ma and I went to said they had rooms available for April 21st, but they said we'd better reserve right away.

When we got in the car after the last hotel, Ma looked at me and said, "Framingham."

"Framingham?" I said. "Ma, Framingham is halfway across the world. Nobody in his right mind would have a bar mitzvah reception forty miles from the temple."

"I know, David. I don't want to look at hotels. I want to check out printers for the invitations. There are a lot more printers in Framingham and I want to price compare. Maybe there will be a big difference in price. Besides, it will be nice to visit civilization."

When Ma says "civilization" she means any town that has its own professional theater group, and doesn't give you parking tickets.

As it turned out there was a big difference in printing prices in Framingham. But it wasn't the kind of difference Ma was looking for. Framingham was more expensive. By the time we'd been to four printers, Ma was feeling kind of down.

"I'm hungry enough to eat a whale," she said.

"Yeah, but where are we going to get a whale?"

"I know where we can get something to eat that's bigger than a whale," Ma said. "Nana's lunch. Let's drop in on Nana and Grampa. We're only fifteen minutes away."

Ma and I played word games on the way to Newton to forget how hungry we were. Nana came to the door and was really happy to see us. But when she found out we hadn't eaten lunch yet she was absolutely beside herself with joy.

43

"So come in, come in. Sit down and I'll fix for you a little something to eat," she said. "Sit down, David. Your grandfather is upstairs taking a nap. Your Aunt Nancy drove him to Boston for his appointment with Dr. Bernstein this morning."

While Ma told Nana what we'd been doing, Nana scurried around the kitchen like a squirrel, taking dishes and bowls out of the cupboard and refrigerator, heating up this, stirring that, slicing something else. In no time at all her kitchen table was covered with enough food to feed an army. There were knishes and *luchen kugel*, which is a kind of noodle pudding, and there was stuffed cabbage and Jewish pastries. These are the things Nana keeps around for an emergency like this. And of course there was Nana's famous chicken soup. While Ma and I ate, Nana sat at the table with us, sipping a cup of black coffee. Nana never eats. She just cooks.

"So what's the matter, David, you don't like the soup?" Nana said, which is what Nana always says if you go more than three seconds without dipping your spoon into the soup.

"Nana, what'cha talkin'? Of course I like it. I'm eating, I'm eating."

"You want some more?"

"In a second, Nana."

"Here." She took my bowl back to the stove and filled it up again.

"Ma, would you please sit down and relax," my mother said. "David will let you know when he wants more food." Ma always gets annoyed when Nana tries to make people eat more than they want.

"So, did you choose a hotel?" Nana said, ignoring Ma.

"Not yet," Ma said. "I can't reserve a room until I have a good idea of how many people are coming. As soon as possible I need a list from you of people you'd like to invite."

"A list? I'll be happy to give you a list. Today," Nana said.

"Good. Michael's mother is sending her list. I hope it's short."

"Well, don't you worry, darling," Nana said, "My list will be short." And even though she's an old woman and she's usually pretty slow, Nana was out of that room like a shot and came back in about two seconds carrying her address book. She put her address book on the table, looked at me suspiciously and said, "More soup?" and grabbed my bowl, but I grabbed the other side before she could get away and after we played tug of war with the bowl for a while she let go and said, "What's the matter with you? You eat like a bird. A growing boy like you, you don't eat enough. What is it? Doesn't you mother feed you?"

"Ma! Stop it!" my mother said. "The list. Let's write the list."

So Nana started going through her address book and calling out names which Ma wrote down on a pad of paper. But all the time Nana kept one eye on me to see what I was eating. I had to be careful. If I ate all the chicken soup in my bowl, Nana would say I must be starving and she'd fill it up again. If I left too much soup in my bowl, she'd say I didn't like it and she'd ask me three hundred times did I think it had too much salt or not enough salt. So I was careful to leave about one spoonful in my second bowl. That's a trick Max Levene taught me

45

and he said that if I did it Nana wouldn't bother me. As long as I kept eating knishes or pastry or something.

After a while Nana's list started to sound like the NBA draft, it was so long. Ma's face was beginning to twitch.

"Myron Feirstein," Nana said, and Ma said, "Who's Myron Feirstein?"

"Feirstein!" Nana said. "Owns the shoe store in Newton Center."

"But he doesn't know David," Ma said. She was getting exasperated.

"What you talking?" Nana said. "The man put the shoes on your little boy's feet for the first three years of his life, till all of you moved out to Westbrick there."

"Westbridge, Mother, bridge, not brick."

"Whatever," Nana said. Then she named a couple of people that Ma had actually heard of and then she said "and don't forget the Stewarts. They're not Jewish, but so what?" and Ma said, "Who are the Stewarts?" and they started all over. Ma's jaw was starting to jut out in a straight line, which is always a bad sign, so I thought it might be a good time for me to go upstairs and visit Max Levene.

When I got upstairs Grampa's bedroom door was open, so I just kind of slipped in quietly. He was stretched out on his bed, still taking a nap. He must have been having a good dream because he was smiling. I stood by his bed for a long time. "Grampa," I called once, but he didn't wake up. I coughed a couple of times, hoping I could accidentally wake him up. I wanted so much to tell him about Kelly. Then I just thought about me and Max and good times we'd had and just looking at him made me smile.

And as I looked at him I noticed something that I had never noticed before. Grampa looked Jewish, whatever that means, and I wondered if I looked Jewish to people, too.

By the time I got back downstairs Ma had switched over to a three-list system. She had a list of people that Nana could definitely invite, a list of people she said Nana could not invite unless we ended up holding the bar mitzvah in Fenway Park, and a list of people she would show to Dad to see if he could figure out who the heck they were.

"Come on, David, get your jacket. We're leaving," Ma said. Her voice was cold as a Popsicle. I could tell that things hadn't gone real well with Nana.

"Oh? Leaving so soon?" Nana said and she came over and gave me a hug. "You're getting big," she said. "A regular man. A bar mitzvah boy, yet."

"Okay," Ma said abruptly. "Thanks for the list. But as I say, it will probably have to be cut. Sorry. I'll get back to you after Michael and I talk it over." She leaned over and gave Nana a little kiss on the cheek.

"Well," Nana said, "just as long as you realize that if you invite Uncle Jacob and Auntie Lillian and don't invite the Goldmans and the Mendelsohns and the Isenbergs, well that whole side of the family will never speak to your father or me again. But . . . it's your decision."

"Oh, Ma. Don't say it like that. It just can't be that bad."

"Oh? So I'm making it up, am I? I'm a liar?"

"Goodbye, Ma," my mother snapped, and we were out the door.

We drove most of the way home in silence. Ma's jaw was jutting out about a mile and she was holding the steering wheel as if she were trying to strangle it.

"What's the problem, Ma?" I said.

"Problem? What problem?"

"Come on, Ma. This is me, David. Your son. The one who knows all about those faces you make. Spill your guts, Ma."

"Well, since you ask . . . it's this bar mitzvah. I don't want the whole thing getting out of hand. I'm afraid that your grandparents will want everybody they know to see your bar mitzvah. I can understand that. But we can't invite the whole world, can we? If we invite everybody they want, then your father and I won't be able to invite the people we want to invite. Do you know how many people in Westbridge are dying to see your bar mitzvah? Most of our friends have never been to a bar mitzvah. It would mean so much to them to see yours. Probably most of the people on your grandparents' lists don't even know you."

"Yes," I said, "and there's another list you haven't even thought about." Now I was getting a little annoyed. "Your son, David's. Remember him?"

"Oh. Oh. Well, sure, David, we wouldn't forget you."

"I get to invite my friends, don't I?"

"David! Of course you do."

"How many?"

"All of your best friends."

"I want to invite the whole eighth grade."

There was a moment of silence.

"But you can't," Ma said. "You just can't."

"Why not?"

"David, I do not believe this."

"Why not?" I said. "You want to invite all your friends and I don't even know half of them."

"David!" Ma was practically screaming now. "I just got through telling you that we can't invite the whole world. Your father is not made out of money, young man."

"It's not fair, Ma."

"*Not fair*? A lot of things are not fair. It's not fair that I have to run all over town trying to make this thing go smoothly."

"Well, if anyone around here should have the right to invite whoever he wants to my bar mitzvah it should be me," I shouted. "I mean, who's bar mitzvah is it, anyway? Is it mine, or is it yours and Dad's?"

My mother gripped the steering wheel tighter and she took three deep breaths, which is her way of telling the world that she's not going to speak a word to anybody ever again or at least for an hour. We drove the rest of the way in a kind of ugly silence, and when we got home I started to dial Kelly's number a couple of times so I could talk to her, but I chickened out.

# Chapter 8

On Halloween I figured I'd be Mr. Nice Guy and take my brother Markie to the party at the school and then take him out to trick-or-treat. Ma wouldn't let him go by himself. Well, God must have been pleased with me, because Kelly was at the party with her little brother and after the party we took them trick-or-treating together. And while the little kids were off ringing doorbells, Kelly and I talked about ghosts and witches and that kind of stuff and she said, "David, is there anything that you're really scared of?"

"I've been scared to ask you to go to the temple with me," I said.

"Why?" she said.

"I don't know. Just afraid that you'd say no, I guess."

"I'll make you a deal," she said. "You ask me to go to the temple with you and I promise I won't say no."

"Will you go to the temple with me?"

"Yes," she said.

It was that easy.

So on Tuesday Ma picked us both up after school. Markie was in the front seat with Ma, so he could go shopping with her while I was having my lesson. If Markie goes more than a week without browsing in the record store in the Searstown Mall he starts to get crazy. Anyhow, Kelly and I got to sit in the back seat close enough for our hands to touch. I wanted to hold her hand but Markie kept turning around about every three seconds.

When we got to the temple Ma drove off quickly with my adorable little brother. Kelly and I walked about half-way down the path to the temple and then she stopped and said, "David, wait. I want to look at it before we go in."

This worried me because there isn't much to look at. I was afraid maybe she was expecting the Taj Mahal or something, and on the outside the temple isn't even fancy like the Catholic church she goes to. It's just a simple building, about the size of a small elementary school, and it sits back from the road between a couple of houses. You could walk by it and not even notice that you did. I thought Kelly was going to say, "It's not what I expected," but all she said was, "Okay. We can go in now."

First you come into a lobby and when we got inside I reached into this wooden box that's always there and I pulled out a yarmulke, a little cap that Jewish men wear. It's about the size of a pancake, but it doesn't fall off unless you lean way over.

"Why are you wearing that?" Kelly asked.

"Have to," I said. "It's to show respect to God."

51

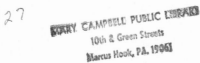

"Should I wear one?"

"Girls don't have to. But you can if you want."

Kelly dug into the pile and pulled out a white yarmulke and popped it on her head.

"It looks good on you," I said, and she giggled.

Then I heard the rabbi call, "David? Is that you?" and he came out of his study and walked toward us. He was carrying a book. Rabbis read a lot. He came up to us and smiled at Kelly and me and I said, "Rabbi, this is Kelly. Kelly, this is Rabbi Kauffman."

"How do you do," he said. He shook Kelly's hand. "Kelly, is it?"

"Uh-huh," Kelly said.

"O'Neil," I said. "She's not Jewish."

It was a dumb thing to say. Kelly's face was suddenly a ripe tomato and I felt like crawling into a hole somewhere.

"Not Jewish?" the rabbi said. "Hmmn," and he shook his head, frowning. "Not a Jewish girl, and with a name like O'Neil, yet. It's hard to figure, you know." He looked us right in the eye.

Kelly and I stared back like a couple of statues and then the rabbi made a big grin and started laughing and then Kelly started laughing, too, and I knew it was okay for me to resume breathing.

"So, Kelly O'Neil, what brings you to Temple Beth-El?" the rabbi said.

"I've never seen the inside of a temple before."

"Ah," the rabbi said, "then you have come to the right place. David, why don't you show your young lady friend around."

"It's all right?" I said. "You don't mind. I mean, my lesson . . ."

"Your lesson will wait for you," he said. "Go ahead. But if you take out the Torah, be very, very careful." He turned to walk back to his study, then he added, "Better, you should come and get me."

I led Kelly all over the place. I took her downstairs to the big room where they have meetings and parties, and sometimes breakfasts. Then I showed her the kitchen, and then I showed her all the classrooms, and when we walked into the classroom where I have my Hebrew lessons Kelly spotted a chart hanging on the wall behind where the rabbi sits.

"I'll bet that's a Hebrew alphabet," she said.

"Lucky guess," I said. "Want to learn it?"

"I'd love to, but it looks hard."

"It's really easy, Kelly, just repeat after me."

So I taught her the first line. And all the time I was showing her the rest of the building Kelly was repeating it, "*aleph, base, vase, gimel, dahlad, hay.*"

When we got outside the room where they hold the religious services, I said, "Ready?"

"For what?" Kelly said.

"For the best part," I said and I yanked open one of the big wooden doors. We walked inside and stood in the center aisle, and Kelly started looking this way and then that way, as if she was lost. I could tell she was impressed because the room has a ceiling like a cathedral and stained glass windows and wooden pews. It probably reminded her of church.

53

"Follow me, young lady," I said, doing an imitation of the rabbi. I took her down to the *bimah*, which is the platform at the front where the rabbi stands during the services. We climbed up the steps.

"This is where the action is, young lady," I said.

"Oh, David!" she said. "It's beautiful in here. Is it all right for us to be up here?"

"Sure," I said. "This is where I'll be standing for my bar mitzvah."

Right then and there I wanted to ask her if she'd come to my bar mitzvah. But then I figured I'd better ask her for a date first.

"See that cranberry-colored curtain?" I said. "That's the Holy Ark."

"You mean like Noah's Ark?" she said.

"No. It's more like a closet that's built into the wall. The Torah is in there."

"Really, David?" She opened her eyes wide and then she said, giggling, "The whole thing? Not just half of it?"

"The whole thing," I said. "Want to see it?"

"Oh, I'd love to."

This was a perfect excuse to touch Kelly, so I took her hand and placed it on the gold cord that pulls open the curtain in front of the ark. "Just pull the curtain open, young lady, and you will see a whole Torah."

"No, David. You do it." I think she was nervous.

"It's okay, Kelly. The Torah has never jumped out and bitten anybody. Go on."

Kelly closed her eyes and gave the cord a tug. The velvety curtains swished to the side, and there was the huge scroll on the shelf, which is also this beautiful cranberry-colored velvet. The Torah is covered with fancy blue velvet cloth and it's decorated with a lot of gold and silver Jewish symbols. Standing there with Kelly, it was like I was seeing it for the first time, too.

"Can I touch it?" she said, and then she reached out and touched the cover very softly as if she were wiping away a tear. Then she looked up to the top of the ark where the Ten Commandments are written in marble, and she gazed at the Eternal Light, which is a lamp made out of fancy brass. It's always lit, and it hangs on a long chain.

"Oh, David, it's so neat here. I love it," Kelly said.

She looked really happy and it seemed like a good time to ask her for a date. I figured she wouldn't turn me down in a temple. But I was scared, and I said, "Thanks. Want to see what a Torah *really* looks like?"

I didn't have to wait for Kelly's answer. It was written all over her face. So I wrapped my arms around the Torah and started lifting it out of the ark.

"Shouldn't you call the rabbi?" Kelly said. "Remember what he said."

"Nah," I said. "He probably thinks it's too heavy for me, but I can do it. Heck, on my bar mitzvah I have to carry it all the way down the aisle."

I got the Torah in my arms and I could feel it slipping. The Torah is almost as big as I am, and it's heavy.

"Can I help you?" Kelly said.

"Hey, no problem," I said. I was being cool. Then I took a couple of steps toward the big table on the *bimah* where they read the Torah and it started slipping toward the floor as if someone were pulling it. I grabbed it real tight near the top, and I pulled up my foot under it to keep it from falling, and like an idiot I started hopping on one foot to the table. Kelly tried not to laugh. And when I finally had the Torah pinned between me and the table, I said, "Boy, they don't make these Torahs like they used to. I guess I could use some help."

The two of us tipped the Torah onto the table. And when it was up there we stayed real close to each other and stared at it. "I guess I'd better get the rabbi," I said, and I ran out of the room.

When we got back the rabbi took the cover off the Torah and unrolled it so that Kelly could see the writing on the parchment and the way it was rolled up on two wooden poles.

"Now," the rabbi said, "since the Torah is opened, there is a law that a *bissell* must be read."

"What's a *bissell*?" Kelly whispered to me.

"It means, 'a little bit'," I said, without really thinking about what I was saying.

"Oh, good, you're going to read some of it, David," she said.

The rabbi smiled.

"I can't," I said. I felt as if I was letting her down, but the rabbi came to my rescue.

"Your David reads his Hebrew very well," he said to Kelly. "But to read the Torah one must study for many, many years. There are no vowels, not even commas, or periods even. Not even music notations."

"*Trope*?" Kelly said.

I couldn't believe she'd remembered.

The rabbi smiled. "Yes, *trope*," he said, "and the Torah is never read, it is always chanted."

"But we're in luck," I said to Kelly. "Because I know someone who can chant the Torah like a pro. Right, Rabbi?"

"Right, David," he said. "Go ahead, sit down, you two. And listen."

Kelly and I sat somewhere in the middle of the synagogue. The room was very quiet, and then it was filled with the the sound of the rabbi chanting the Hebrew from the Torah. I was thinking that I wanted to hold Kelly's hand, and she must have been thinking the same thing, because all of a sudden, there we were, holding hands. We sat very still as we watched the rabbi sway and sing and pray on the *bimah*. I felt a chill. It was like something was tickling me deep inside. I looked at Kelly. Her eyes were all misty. She leaned over to me and she squeezed my hand and she said, "David, if I wasn't Catholic I think I'd be Jewish," and then she turned and looked straight at the rabbi until he was done chanting.

Kelly stayed in the synagogue while I had my Hebrew lesson, and when Ma dropped her off later I walked her to the door.

"David, thank you so much for taking me to the temple," she said. "I'm going to tell everybody about it."

"Do you think . . ." I said. My heart was thumping.

"Do I think what?"

"Do you think we could go out on a date sometime?"

"A date?" she said, as if she was surprised I asked.

I nodded.

"David, you're so silly," she said. "We just went out on one."

# *Chapter 9*

The next day when I got home from school there was a note from Ma saying she had to go to Newton and she'd be home late. Markie and I made supper.

Supper was ready when Ma came in. She looked worn out. "Is your father home?" is all she said. I told her Dad was in the family room and she walked straight in there. After about fifteen minutes they both came out and we all sat down to supper.

Supper went okay except that Ma and Dad seemed kind of quiet, and when we were all scraping at the bottom of our desserts and loosening our belt buckles, Dad leaned back in his chair and said, "Well, Markie, you did a great job setting the table. Now I think I'd like to hear you play the piano. How about singing me that new song you've been working on."

I couldn't believe it. Usually after supper Dad says something like, "I'm going to catch the seven o'clock news. You boys will be peaceful and quiet, and there will be no piano playing. Thank you."

After Dad and Markie went into the living room Ma asked me to help her clear the table, which I did. But when I noticed that she wasn't putting on her Playtex rubber gloves I figured she had her eye on somebody else for dish detail, so I started to sneak off to my room to practice my haftorah.

Before I even got to the stairs, Ma called, "David, don't leave. I have to talk to you, honey."

I don't know if I have psychic powers or if it was just the way Ma said it, but right then I knew my life was about to get clobbered.

"What about, Ma? What's wrong?" I sort of shouted it and Ma winced. Sometimes when I get worried I sound as if I'm mad even though I'm really just scared.

Ma turned and walked back into the kitchen, kind of wringing her hands. I followed her in there. She stared around as if what she had to tell me was printed on one of the walls and she just had to find it.

"I spoke to Grampa's doctor today," she said.

"So?" I said. "Did you have a nice chat?" My heart started beating fast.

"David, you know Grampa's been tired a lot since his heart attack."

"Sure," I said. "But that was a year ago. He's getting better."

"No," my mother said. She looked like she wanted to cry. "Grampa is not getting better. David, sometimes when you get old your arteries start to deteriorate . . . I mean, they get weak . . . and . . ."

"Well, sure," I said. "He's an old guy. But don't you worry about Max Levene. He'll . . ."

"David! His heart isn't very strong right now, either. He doesn't have to go to the hospital or anything like that, but he does have to take it easy."

"Oh," I said. I could feel my throat getting dry and it was like my words had to crawl out. "I'll give old Max a call and tell him to forget about the tryout with the Celtics," I said.

"David," Ma blurted out, "the doctors are afraid Grampa might not make it much past February."

I didn't know what to say. It was like I'd always known that sooner or later something really horrible would happen to me and now here it was. Like a monster had been chasing me all my life and now had caught up with me. Ma pulled me into her arms and held me and rubbed my back and my hair the way she always used to. I felt like a little kid.

"Grampa is dying, Ma?" I finally whispered.

"Yes."

I tried to hold in my tears, but they came out anyhow, little drops of warm water running down my cheeks. Ma held me tight and I cried. Grampa. He was the only person that it was easy to say I loved. I didn't want him to die.

I don't know how long we stood there in the kitchen. I could hear Markie in the living room whacking away at the piano and I remembered that it was Grampa who bought the piano, and after a while it was like everything I could think of had something to do with Grampa.

"David," I heard my mother say. "There is something very special we could do for Grampa. Something special that *you* could do."

60

Ma pressed her fingers under my chin and made me look her in the face even though my eyes were full of tears.

I wiped my eyes with my sleeve. "What?"

"Your bar mitzvah."

"What about it?" I said. I was getting scared, but I didn't know why.

"We could move it up for Max."

"Move it up?" I said. "To when?"

"To your birthday."

"December?"

"Yes."

"But, Ma, that's crazy. What about the weather? You remember what you said."

Ma smiled and she put on a certain face that she puts on when she thinks she's doing an impression of me. "The heck with the weather, ya know!" she said.

"No, Ma," I cried. "I can't." I was getting panicky. "Don't ask me to do that. There's not enough time to learn all the stuff I have to learn. I need the six months. Besides doctors don't know anything. Max won't die before I have my bar mitzvah. He'll probably live another ten years. I read about a guy once, the doctors said he had six months to live, and the guy was still alive and it had been four years and . . ."

"David! You could do it, honey, I know you could. You could study every day. The rabbi will help you. I know he will."

I stepped back from Ma. I wasn't even used to the idea of Grampa dying yet and here she was pressuring me to do things I knew I couldn't do.

"Every day?" I said. "What about schoolwork? What about Shrimp League?"

"You'll work it out, David. You always do."

"Ma, it can't be done," I shouted.

"You can do it," she pleaded.

"No," I said. "I can't. Nobody could. I know what you want. You want me to have my bar mitzvah before Grampa dies so he can be there and see me. I understand, Ma, I do, but it's just too . . ."

I don't know what I was going to say, but just then it hit me that what Ma wanted wasn't just insane. It was impossible.

"What about the haftorah?" I said.

"What about it?" Ma said. She looked startled.

"I've been memorizing it for more than a month already. That will be a waste. If I'm bar mitzvahed in December the rabbi will be at a different place in the Torah."

Ma's face went white. "Oh, David, you're right. You'll have to learn a new haftorah."

"Yeah," I snapped, "and I wouldn't even have two months to learn it. Don't you see? Ma, I've been practicing. I've been singing into the tape recorder and everything."

Ma didn't say anything. She just stepped back and leaned against the sink. Her body kind of sunk and her hands just hung by her sides. I thought for sure she had given up on this crazy idea of me being bar mitzvahed on my birthday. But then the tears started coming into her eyes. "Oh, David," she cried, "he's my father and he's dying and it would mean so much to him to see your bar mitzvah. You have to do this for me."

"No, Ma," I said. I was so angry. Grampa was dying

and I didn't even want to be bar mitzvahed in the first place and here she was trying to make it harder and harder on me, so I'd have to give up basketball completely and Kelly and everything. "*No*," I shouted. "I'm sorry. You're asking too much," and I stomped out of the kitchen and ran up to my room and slammed the door.

# Chapter 10

For a few days Ma and I acted as if nothing had happened. We talked about the bar mitzvah, but neither one of us said anything about when it would be. It was as if Ma was waiting for me to give in and say, "Okay, Ma, you win. December will be wonderful!" and I was waiting for her to say, "You're right, David, December's impossible, April will be fine." Neither one of us budged.

But no matter when the bar mitzvah was going to be, no sane person would expect me to stay in my room and chant Hebrew into a tape recorder on a Sunday afternoon when the Celtics were playing the Philadelphia 76ers on television. Ma told me to take the day off so I could watch the basketball game with Dad and my Uncle Danny, who's married to Ma's sister Nancy. Then Ma announced that she was "on strike," which meant that she was taking the day off, too. Only Ma is always dramatic about it and she came into the family room where we all were and she said, "Your attention please. I have an announcement. I am on strike today. Gentlemen who wish to eat will proceed to the kitchen and cook their own food.

"Besides," she added, "I have company of my own coming. Danny's bringing Nana and Grampa."

"Grampa?" I said. I was startled to hear he was coming. I hadn't seen him since I'd heard the news.

"Yes, David," Ma said. "What's wrong?"

"Nothing," I said, but my heart was pounding. I didn't know how I should act with Grampa, what I should say.

But when Grampa came in, he acted as if everything was fine. Ma had told Danny she was on strike so he and Grampa and Nana had stopped at the Jewish delicatessen in Newton and they came in with a bunch of white bags.

"Ah, David," Grampa said. "You like corned beef?" He led me into the kitchen, but he moved very slowly. "We got corned beef. And we got salami and sour tomatoes." He put his bags on the kitchen table. "How about potato salad? Anybody here who doesn't like potato salad? It doesn't matter, you should have a little lox and cream cheese on a nice bagel. Sour pickles? Rolled beef? Bulkie rolls? Whatever you should want."

I didn't know exactly what I should say to Grampa so I said what everybody says, "How are you feeling?"

Grampa smiled. "I'm feeling like an old man," he said. "How should I feel?"

"I don't know," I said. "I was worried that . . ."

"David," he said and he patted my shoulder, "you're twelve years old. You shouldn't worry."

So we all sat down in the family room and pigged out on delicatessen food while we watched the Celtics game.

Of course, not all of us were fanatical Celtics fans, so there was a lot of talking going on, which is okay during the first quarter, but it can drive you nuts later in the game. As usual, Nana kept wondering out loud how come we all liked to watch a bunch of grown men run around in shorts. "It's *meshugge*," she said, which means, "it's crazy."

And good old Max Levene wouldn't know a jump shot from a full-court press, so he kept watching our faces to see if we were happy, or not so happy, about what was going on. If we cheered because Danny Ainge or one of the other Celtics scored, Max would say, "It's good, what he did?" and if we booed because Moses Malone slam-dunked the ball while three guys were covering him, Max would say, "This is not so good, huh?"

By the end of the first quarter the Celtics were behind by three points, we were all stuffed and Max Levene was nodding off. Ma helped him upstairs and made him take a nap. And Nana, who gets edgy as heck when she goes more than two hours without cooking something, went into the kitchen and started poking around.

The second quarter was even more tragic. Andrew Toney kept popping in his fade-away jump shot, which he never seems to miss when he's playing the Celtics, and Robert Parish couldn't seem to pick off any rebounds. It looked like the Celtics were going to be down by ten points at half-time, but when there was just one second to go in the half, Larry Bird launched this incredible desperation hook shot from half court, and Dad and Danny and I all leaned forward at the same time and shouted, "Good if it goes," not that we figured there was any chance of the shot going in. But the shot swished right through the basket and we all cheered and everybody in the Boston Garden cheered and even though the Celtics were down by seven points, it made everybody a lot happier at half-time.

"What does that mean?" Markie asked me while Dad and Uncle Danny were out in the kitchen getting beer for the second half.

"What?" I said.

"'Good if it goes'?"

I couldn't believe it. Markie never asks me anything about basketball. He doesn't usually like sports, and when we're watching a game he mostly just hangs around and draws pictures or something.

"Well, it means the basket is good if the ball goes in even though the time period is over," I explained. "As long as you get the shot off before the buzzer, and nobody else touches it, the basket counts."

"Oh," he said, and he started singing it as if it was a song. Everything is a song to Markie. That's when he asked me if he could borrow my tape recorder sometime. I should have said no, but I said okay, figuring Markie's a pretty good kid sometimes.

Of course Markie isn't the only weirdo who likes to draw pictures while normal people are watching basketball games. Right after the third quarter started, Ma came marching into the family room with her sketch pad and pencils. She dropped a yarmulke on my head and wrapped Dad's *tallis* around my shoulder. A *tallis* is a white silk shawl that Jewish men wear when they're praying, and I'd be wearing one for my bar mitzvah. Then Ma

67

sat beside me on the couch and said, "Do not move for the next half-hour, David, or I'll give you back to the Gypsies who left you on my doorstep so many years ago."

"Cute, Ma, cute," I said. "What's going on?"

"Sit still," she said, and she pulled her knees up and started sketching on her pad. "Do not move. I repeat, do not move."

"I'm not moving," I said. "What's up?"

"I'm drawing your portrait for the front of the bar mitzvah invitations," she said.

Oh, oh, I thought. Here it comes. She's going to bring up this business of switching the bar mitzvah to December 17th, my birthday. But she didn't. At least, not exactly. She just said, "I've got to get this to the printer this week, and this is my only chance to draw you. It seems the only person who can get you to sit in one place for an hour is Larry Bird."

"Great material, Ma. Maybe you could get on *Saturday Night Live*.

"Don't move."

"I'm not, I'm not."

"Well, don't. Just watch the game. Do not move, do not pass 'Go,' do not collect two hundred dollars."

So between Ma's awful jokes and the fact that I had to stay as still as a corpse, I watched the third quarter in a lot of pain. Not only that, but the Celtics played so bad that I think the Marlboro Dwarfs could have beat them, and the Dwarfs were in last place in the Shrimp League.

By the start of the fourth period the Celtics were doing so terribly that the Philadelphia players were getting bored, and Ma was carrying on as if the fate of the entire world depended on her finishing the sketch of me. But then she heard the bedroom door upstairs and when she saw Max Levene starting down the stairs after his nap, she dropped her pencil and pad so fast you'd have thought they were on fire and she dashed up to help him. She led him into the kitchen and they sat around drinking coffee with Nana. I couldn't believe it. One minute she was totally concentrating on me for the portrait, the next minute she was gone, like a ship that had sunk without a trace.

Sometimes when I'm watching a basketball game and the Celtics aren't doing so well I lose track of the game and start thinking about other things while I'm still staring at the TV screen. It's like a trance. So with the Celtics playing like a bunch of three-legged donkeys, I started thinking mostly about the way Ma ditched me the minute Max Levene showed up. And after a while I felt kind of dumb for being angry with Ma because I realized that she was worried about her father and probably wanted to spend as much time with him as she could, because nobody knew how much time was left. And I realized something else weird. I had been avoiding Grampa. I had hardly even talked to him, even though I could have told him about Kelly and lots of other things. Mostly, I guess I didn't know what to say to him. I mean I knew about doctors being wrong most of the time, and I wanted to tell him about this guy who had lived for ten years after the doctors had said he was a goner, but it seemed like you weren't even supposed to bring up the subject in front of everybody.

I went on staring at the TV screen and thinking like that until I heard my Uncle Danny say, "Tradition," and it kind of woke me up because I figured he and Dad must be talking about my bar mitzvah.

"Huh?" I said.

"Tradition," Uncle Danny said, and he waved his beer can toward the TV screen. It was timeout in the game and the camera was showing all the Celtics' championship flags. The Celtics have won thirteen world championships and for each one they have a green and white banner hanging from the top of the Boston Garden, where they play.

"What do you mean?" I said.

Danny turned to my father. "Hey, Mike, don't you tell your kids anything? I mean we're only talking here about the greatest team in the history of sports." Danny grew up in Boston and he's been a Celtics fan since he was my age.

"Except the New York Yankees," my father said, because he grew up in New York.

"Ah, foreigners!" Uncle Danny said. "Look, David," he said, "how many Celtics do you think have won scoring championships in the past twenty-five years?"

"I don't know. Ten?" I guessed.

"Zip," Danny said. "Not a one. You know why?"

"Why?"

"Because they want to win basketball games, not scoring championships. See, most teams have one guy who can score 35 points a game. Not the Celtics. But they've always had a guy who could score 25 points a game, and another guy who could score 22 points and a couple of guys who could score 18 points a game and maybe three more guys who were good for 10 or 12 points. You know what I mean?"

"Yeah," I said.

"And never giving up," Danny said, "that's part of their tradition, too. I remember one game, when I was a kid, the Celtics were down by 10 points with one minute to go. One minute! And they won the game. It seemed impossible for them to win, but they won the game, anyway. They just didn't give up. Teamwork did it. That's their tradition. The older guys pass it on to the new guys, and that's how they managed to win thirteen world championships."

"That's tradition?" I said.

Danny laughed. "It is when you've been doing it as long as they have," he said.

"I wonder what they would have been like without tradition," I said.

"They wouldn't have been the Celtics," he said. "They'd've been just a bunch of guys playing basketball."

I guess I hadn't ever really thought about a basketball team having traditions. But what Uncle Danny said kind of made sense, the way that what Grampa said about throwing sticks into the stream made sense. Tradition. For the first time, it wasn't just a word. I thought about it for a while.

What Grampa said down by the stream made me realize why my bar mitzvah seemed so important to everybody. I closed my eyes and pictured myself standing up there on the *bimah* in the temple, looking out at everybody. Suddenly, I realized that Max Levene really might not be there, and I felt a hard lump in my throat and my chest felt so heavy that I had to take a couple of slow, deep breaths.

71

Grampa had to be at my bar mitzvah, I thought, he just had to be. I knew I would have to move it up to my birthday, even if it did seem impossible. Ma had said the rabbi would help me, and I really would have to study every day. But it was the only way. I would just have to do it. Then I realized that I believed in tradition all along. I just never knew it.

I thought about this for a couple of minutes, and then I went into the kitchen. Ma and Nana and Grampa were sitting at the table eating an apple pie that Nana had baked.

"How are the Celtics doing?" my mother asked.

"Ma," I said, "do you know the meaning of the word *disgraceful*?"

"That bad, huh?"

"Yeah. It's not quite over yet. I just came out here to see if Max Levene has a snow shovel."

"A snow shovel?" Grampa said. "This is something you need right now in the middle of a basketball game?"

"No, Max Levene," I said. "You're going to need it. I'm changing my bar mitzvah to December 17th and there will probably be a blizzard, so you'd better be ready to shovel your way to the temple because we're not going to have it without you."

My mother just said, "David," very softly, and me and Max Levene hugged for a long time, but I still didn't know what else to say to him.

# Chapter 11

The rabbi sent for my new haftorah right away, and I started going to Hebrew school every single day for two weeks. By the time Thanksgiving vacation rolled around, I was ready to pull my hair out. So when I got out of school that Wednesday afternoon, I felt as if I'd been released from the state prison. And the best thing about that Wednesday was that I got to play in a Midgets game. Once the weather got too cold to play outdoors, the Midgets games switched from Tuesdays to Wednesdays because that was the day the Catholic church said we could use the St. John's gym. The worst thing about that Wednesday was that I played as if I'd just landed from Uranus or someplace and had never actually seen a basketball before. After a while everybody stopped passing to me. Not that I blame them. I wouldn't have passed to me either. Through some miracle the Midgets had managed to get into a tie for first place in the Shrimp League, but my performance helped push them back into second.

When I trudged through the door that night, having personally led my team to a stunning defeat, I was not in what anybody would call a really great mood.

Ma had kept supper warm while everybody waited for me to get home, so I had to sit through the meal even though I was about as anxious to eat as I was to have my gall bladder removed. I stabbed at the meatloaf and flattened the potatoes with my fork to make it look as if there was something going on in the area of my plate.

"David, you're not eating," my mother said.

"I'm not hungry."

"Well, you should eat anyway. All that exercise."

"Some exercise!" I said. "Throwing the ball out of bounds. Missing easy layups."

"You should be starving."

"Well, I'm not starving," I snapped.

"Watch it, young man," my father said. "Don't be fresh."

I looked down at the table. "I'm not hungry."

"Is something wrong?" Ma asked. "What is it?"

"Nothing's wrong," I said, even though the truth is that everything was wrong. I poked at my food some more.

"David," Ma said, "if something is bothering you and you don't talk about it, it won't go away, you know. Do you want to talk about it?" Ma put down her fork and waited for an answer.

"There's nothing to talk about," I said. Then I squinted my eyes and made my voice sound real nasty and I hissed, "May I be excused?"

I could feel my father glaring at me from across the table. "Watch that attitude of yours, young man," he said.

74

"What attitude?" I shouted. "I don't have an attitude." It was getting pretty obvious that the whole world was out to get me. I wanted to be alone.

Dad looked disgusted with me. "That's it. Go to your room," he said.

I stood up and pushed back my chair. Neither my mother nor my father would look at me, so I looked at Markie and said, "All right, I'm going, I'm going."

When I got upstairs I grabbed my basketball, the only real friend I had left in the house, and I started dribbling on the floor. In about ten seconds there was a very hard knock on my door.

"David? What are you doing?" It was my father.

"Nothing."

"Nothing?" he shouted. "The whole house is shaking."

"I'm bouncing my basketball, that's all," I said.

"David, I'm coming in," he said, and he pushed open my door and came in and said, "Let's get something straight, young man. Your bedroom is not St. John's gym. Do you understand?"

I didn't answer.

"David?"

"Yes, sir," I said.

And then instead of being angry with me Dad just kind of looked at me, all full of pity as if I were some bum on the street who had asked him for a dime. "Let's talk," he said, and he sat on my bed and patted the spot next to him for me to sit there.

"You've been under a lot of pressure lately," he said.

"Well, well, you noticed."

"Of course I've noticed," he said. "We've all noticed.

Don't forget, I went through this once myself." He laughed. "Of course that was about three hundred years ago, but I still remember."

"Dad," I said, "these last couple of weeks have been the worst of my life. Nothing but work, work, work. I can't take it anymore."

Dad doesn't usually hug me as much as Ma does, but he put his arm around me and after a few minutes of neither one of us speaking he said, "Did you get to speak to Kelly today?"

Kelly. Just hearing her name made me smile. "No," I said. "Her family goes away for Thanksgiving. They're going to Pawtucket, Rhode Island. Can you imagine anybody going to Pawtucket, Rhode Island, voluntarily?"

"No." Dad laughed. "There are a lot of strange things in the world, aren't there?"

"Yeah."

"Well, you did get to play basketball today," he said. "I'll bet that was fun, for a change."

"Some fun!" I said.

"What happened?"

"I don't think I even want to talk about it," I said.

"That bad?"

"Dad," I said, "do you know the meaning of the word *stunk*? *S-T-U-N-K*?"

"Hmmn," he said. "When I was a kid it wasn't very good."

"Well, it's no better now," I said, and we both laughed, though I still felt pretty awful.

"You're just out of practice," Dad said. "You've been so

busy with everything else. The kids understand. You had an off day."

"Come on, Dad. When you're out on the court no one cares about your problems, you know that. They only know that you let them down."

"Is that how you feel? That you let them down?"

"It's not just the way I feel," I said. "It's the way it is. I *did* let them down. Dad, I usually score from way outside. Today I couldn't even score a layup."

"I can tell you feel lousy," he said. "But there will be other games. You'll get your eye back. Even Larry Bird has a bad day now and then."

I knew he was trying to make me feel better. And it helped. But not much.

Dad stood up. "I ran into Jim Bellarosa the other day," he said. "He asked me if you were going out for the school team."

Mr. Bellarosa is the basketball coach at the junior high school. "I couldn't make that team, Dad. I'm practically the shortest kid in the school."

"He said he thought you had a chance."

"Really?" I said.

"Really."

"He probably tells all the parents that."

"I don't think so. Some of the kids told him you were pretty good. He said maybe he could use you in the back court. Probably second string, though."

I knew that even if I did make the team I'd spend most of my time sitting on the bench. But that was okay. At least I'd be playing on a team with uniforms and referees and real fans cheering. "What's the difference?" I said. "Even if I could make the team, and I probably couldn't, I wouldn't be able to play in any games, going to Hebrew school every day."

"Your bar mitzvah's December 17th," Dad said. "There's only one junior-high-school game before then. All the rest come later."

"How do you know?" I said.

"I checked," he said. He smiled. "You know, in case I ran into anybody who was interested in that sort of thing."

"Thanks, Dad," I said. I couldn't believe it. One more thing to think about.

"It's up to you, David," he said, "but if you decide you want to go to basketball tryouts I'll pull some strings to see that you get out of going to Hebrew school that day. And another thing, young man, the reason you didn't do well today is that you've been under all this pressure. Hebrew school. Grampa. It's a lot for anybody. Don't be so hard on yourself, okay?"

"Okay," I said.

He gave me a little hug. "I'm going now. Why don't you work on your haftorah a little bit tonight and take tomorrow off. Your mother's making a nice Jewish dinner for Thanksgiving. Turkey with stuffing, cranberry sauce, mashed potatoes, turnips. You know, Jewish food!"

"Dad?" I said before he left.

"What?"

"Do you think Kelly would go with me?"

"Go where with you?"

"You know. Go with me?"

"Oh," he said. "We used to call it going steady."

"Yeah."

"I think so," he said. "But there's one very hard thing you have to do first."

"What?"

"You have to ask her," he said.

I was feeling a lot better after Dad left, even though the idea of asking Kelly to go with me was practically making me sick. I found my new haftorah buried under a pile of school papers, but I couldn't find my tape recorder. Then I went downstairs to look for it and I found it on the piano bench. The rabbi had made a recording of my new haftorah so I could play it over and over while I read along. The tape was still in the recorder.

I went back up to my room and closed the door. I plugged in the tape recorder and sat on my bed and stared into my haftorah booklet. I was finally starting to calm down. Then the rabbi's voice came on, chanting, "VA YIK R'VU Y'MAY DOVID LO MUS, VAI TSAV ES SHLO-MO V'NO LAY- MOR . . ." I followed in the book and sang along with the tape.

Then it happened. Suddenly the rabbi's voice got high-pitched and he was singing in English. I couldn't believe it. Then I heard the piano. Then I heard the drums. Then I heard the guitar. Then I knew. It was Popcorn, singing one of Markie's dumb songs. On my tape.

I snapped. I tore out of my room and flew down the stairs, screaming with each step, *Markie, you're going to get it.*

Everyone came running into the downstairs hall. Ma looked frightened. "What is it?" she said. My father was right behind her with his arms folded like a general's. "What's the problem?" he said.

"*Markie*," I said. "He's my problem. But he's not going to be for long. I'm really going to give it to him this time." I made a leap for Markie and he ran behind Ma. "Let me at him," I screamed, "let me at him."

"Stop it, David, stop it," my mother cried. My father grabbed me around the waist but I kept flailing my arms, figuring I could at least grab a chunk of Markie's hair or an ear or something.

"Let me go, Dad, let me at him. He ruined it. Ruined it."

"Ruined what? What are you talking about?"

"My haftorah!" I said. "The tape the rabbi made. That's what. It's ruined. That stupid little pain taped right over it with his stupid singing group. Popcorn. I'm going to wring all of their necks."

"We did not tape over it!" Markie shouted. "I used my own tape."

"You didn't use your own tape, you creep. You used mine and I can prove it."

"It was an accident then," Markie said. "I didn't mean it. I'm sorry." He burst into tears, but I didn't care, I wanted to whack him good. Dad finally let me go, then he and Ma ran over to Markie because he was crying like a baby. I felt as if I wasn't even there.

"Damn," I screamed. "Don't you realize that I only have about three weeks left to learn that thing? And more besides. You don't even care, do you? You just don't care."

80

Ma's eyes were filled with horror. "Oh David, how can you say such a thing? Of course we care."

Dad took my arm and pulled me over to the stairway. "Look," he said, "you're upset now. We all understand that. Go to your room and try to calm down. Go on. We'll talk about this later."

Calm down? My insides were on fire. I stood there on the bottom step, glaring at everybody. Then I started up the stairs and I turned around and hollered, "You bet I'm going to my room. And remember, it's *my* room." Then I ran up the rest of the stairs two at a time, wishing Kelly was home so I could call her.

# Chapter *12*

The next morning I was a lot calmer. I woke up to the smell of pancakes. When I got downstairs the dining room table was set. There were even flowers.

"Special *breakfast* for Thanksgiving, too?" I said.

"No," Ma said. "Special breakfast for the bar mitzvah boy."

"Me?"

"Yes," she laughed. "Your father and I know you've been working hard for your bar mitzvah and we want you to know we appreciate it."

After I finished eating my first stack, Ma said, "And by the way, David, if you think you might like to take Kelly to the movies this weekend, I'll be glad to drive you."

So Friday morning I phoned Kelly and asked her for a date.

I had figured it this way. I'd take her out and I'd ask her if she'd go with me, or "go steady," as Dad would say. If she said yes, I wouldn't have to worry about whether or not she liked some boy better than she liked me . . . I had enough to worry about . . . and I'd be happy for the rest of my days. Or at least for the rest of the night. And if things went really rotten and she said no, then I wouldn't even care about the rest of my days and I knew for a fact that I'd spend the rest of the night, anyway, throwing up. So when I phoned her and asked her if she'd go to the movies with me, Saturday night, she said yes, not knowing that she'd be going on a date with an absolute wreck of a man. Well, almost a man.

On Saturday night Ma drove us to the Searstown Mall, where there's a pizza place and seven movie theaters. Kelly and I sat in the back seat and I kept her talking all the way, talking about basketball, kids at school, little brothers, anything to keep her from noticing the pile of junk on the floor of Ma's car. I wanted to impress Kelly, not make her nauseous.

Ma dropped us off at the pizza place and said she'd be back at eleven to pick us up. There was a long line at the counter so Kelly and I had to stand and wait. I was sorry we had talked so much in the car. It seemed as if there was nothing left to talk about except what kind of pizza to get. We settled on a plain pizza and a pitcher of root beer, which was good because plain pizza is the cheapest and I didn't have much money.

Kelly picked out a booth near the door. I figured that proved she was proud to be seen with me. But it was getting so everything she did meant something, or at least I hoped it did.

It was time to ask the big question. I waited until Kelly had wolfed down two slices of pizza. Then I spoke.

"Great pizza, huh?" I said. I figured I'd lead up to the big question slowly.

"Umm," she said. She picked up another slice.

"Yeah, I really love the pizza here," I said. I was feeling really witty. "I come here all the time." I went on with a few other brilliant remarks like that, then I said, "Of course I haven't been here lately. Been too busy. But this is a special occasion." I picked up my glass of root beer and gulped it down.

"Special occasion?" Kelly said. "What do you mean?"

"Huh?" I said. "Oh, nothing. Just, uh . . . you know . . ." I laughed, "a special occasion," and I quickly poured some more root beer into my glass and gulped that down, practically breaking a tooth on an ice cube.

"David, what's going on with you lately, anyhow?"

"What do you mean?" I said. My hands were shaking.

"You seem nervous, and Jennifer says she never sees you go home on the bus anymore." Then she frowned. "And you don't call me very much."

"I'm sorry," I said. "It's just that I've been going to Hebrew school every day."

"Why?" she said. "I thought two days a week was plenty."

"It was," I said. I was starting to calm down, and I wasn't thinking about asking the big question. "But my bar mitzvah's been moved up."

"Moved up?"

"Yeah. It's going to be December 17th."

"But that's next month," Kelly said. "Why?"

"Oh, it's nothing," I said. "Just that some doctors made a mistake. They think my grandfather might die before

84

April and so my mother wanted to have it in December just to be sure he'd see it."

"Oh, David."

"I'm not worried," I said. "It's no big deal. You know how doctors are. They think everybody is dying."

"What's wrong with your grandfather?"

"They say his heart is really weak, and his arteries, too. But they don't know Max Levene the way I know him. He's strong. He'll fool them. I know he will."

"Max Levene?"

"That's my grandfather. I call him Max Levene."

"I guess I know how you feel," Kelly said. "My grandmother died last year. We were really close. Are you close to you grandfather?"

"Max Levene? Are you kidding? He's the greatest. Max and I are real buddies. Someday you'll meet him."

"I'd really like to," Kelly said softly and she placed her hand right on top of mine. "If you'd like." Then Kelly gave my hand a squeeze and she said, "You know, David, if you ever want to talk about stuff like this. Or just, you know, . . . anything . . . you can call me."

It was the perfect time for me to say, "Kelly, will you go with me?" but when I opened my mouth nothing would come out. So I grabbed my root beer glass quickly and waved it at her and smiled and I gulped down the root beer and stared at Kelly through the bottom of the glass. She smiled back at me.

When I plopped my glass back on the table, Kelly said, "Boy, you sure must have been thirsty." She peeked into the pitcher. "Nothing left but foam! You can finish mine."

# Chapter *13*

During Hebrew school on Monday the rabbi made another tape for me. He taped my new haftorah again, the one Popcorn had erased from the face of the earth, and he also taped the *maftir* for the day of my bar mitzvah. The *maftir* is the last sentences that are read from the Torah during services, and the bar mitzah boy doesn't *have* to read them, but everybody is impressed and proud as heck if he does.

After Hebrew school, Ma dropped me off at the basketball court, then went home to work some more on the invitations. She knew I was hoping I could get into the playoff game the Midgets would have if they finished in the top four. And, also, the eighth-grade team tryouts were only a week away. So I wanted to work on my long shots. When I got home for supper Ma was in the kitchen and the kitchen smelled delicious.

"Chili," she said, and she smiled as if she had gotten away with something wicked.

"Chili?" I said. "Dad hates chili."

"I know," she said. "That's why I sent him off to McDonald's with Markie. I told them not to come back for a couple of hours because you and I were going to be busy eating chili." She smiled and poked a finger in the air. "Plus, if you act now, at no extra cost . . . garlic bread!"

"Garlic bread? Ma, you're a genius."

"I know," she said. "Now wash up for supper."

When I got back downstairs Ma had put out the chili and garlic bread on the dining room table. There were candles on it, too.

"By candlelight we're eating?" I said.

"That's right. We deserve something special. We've both been knocking ourselves out lately for this bar mitzvah. Besides, it isn't every day that I get a chance to dine alone with a handsome gentleman." She handed me a book of matches. "Would you light the candles, monsieur."

"Getting sentimental in your old age, Ma?" I said.

"Could be," she said. She kissed my cheek and I lit the candles. Ma had put out the good dishes, crystal glasses and cloth napkins, which she always folds up so that they look like flowers.

I poured some soda for myself and I got Ma's favorite white wine. "Chablis for the lady?" I said. I was actually feeling happy, and trying not to think about the fact that I'd have to go upstairs later and study my haftorah.

"Why, thank you, kind sir," my mother said. I was tempted to ask her if her accent was supposed to be British or Hungarian, but I figured she'd shove an elbow into my ribs.

"I hope it meets with madam's approval."

"Indeed," she said, and she sipped the wine. "Dry, light, just about perfect," she said. Sometimes Ma sounds a lot like a TV commercial.

Then we got down to the serious business of digging into our chili. You'd think neither one of us had eaten for three weeks, the way we went at it. After we'd both gone through our first helpings in record time, Ma said, "Congratulate me."

"What for?"

"I'll be able to mail off the last batch of bar mitzvah invitations tomorrow."

"Congratulations," I said. Ma had been addressing envelopes for days. The reason it took so long is that Ma thought my bar mitzvah invitations should be works of art that would last longer than the Mona Lisa, so she had printed them in calligraphy, which is a very fancy kind of handwriting that looks great, but takes forever to do.

"More chili?" Ma said, and she started heaping some more into my bowl. "Of course, the invitations are going out much too late, but almost everyone knows when the bar mitzvah is, so I guess it's okay."

For a while Ma kept talking about the bar mitzvah. She looked real tired suddenly. It's not surprising. Changing the date of a bar mitzvah is like trying to launch a space shuttle way ahead of schedule. In the first place, Ma had finally made reservations to use the big banquet room at the Sheraton Hotel in Boxborough for the reception on April 21st. Then, when things changed, Ma had to call them up and cancel. She tried to make a reservation for December 17th, but they said forget it, lady, we're all

90

booked up. So Ma called another hotel. And another. And another. And about ten more, and there weren't any decent rooms available for the reception, except maybe in Ohio. Then she cried for a while and, finally, called the rabbi to see if we could have the reception downstairs in the temple. The rabbi said fine, but the food would have to be kosher. Kosher is kind of hard to explain, especially when you don't completely understand it, the way I don't. But basically it means that food has to be cooked a certain way and in a specially prepared place that has been blessed and you only use certain dishes and knives and forks. It's complicated and the rabbi said Ma would either have to prepare the food in the temple, or get a certified kosher caterer. Well, Ma had a kosher caterer all right, but she wasn't certified. It was Nana and she and Ma were going to have to do all the cooking in the temple. So Ma started planning the food for two hundred people. Then, of course, the invitations had to be hurried up. So Ma had made the sketch of me, wearing a yarmulke and my father's *tallis*, had gone to the printers, and then had addressed all those envelopes in calligraphy, and God knows what else. All in no time. No wonder she was exhausted.

"I talked to your grandfather today," Ma said. She was still talking about the bar mitzvah when I finished my second bowl of chili. "He spoke to his friend who makes the yarmulkes. We should have them all about a week before the big day."

"Will my name really be on them?"

"Sure," Ma said, beaming proudly. "Right on the lining. 'Bar Mitzvah of David Scott Newman.' My son! And the

91

date will be printed, too. They'll make great souvenirs. And, let's see, we have to get you a *tallis*. Probably nothing fancy. The only place you can get a really special one is New York." She laughed. "Or Israel, I suppose."

"Ma," I said, "you don't have to buy me a *tallis*. I'll wear Dad's." I was getting worried about how much money she and Dad were spending on my bar mitzvah. It seemed crazy. I wondered how many season tickets to the Celtics you could buy with the money.

"Don't be silly," my mother said. "The bar mitzvah boy should have his own *tallis*, even if it's not a fancy one. Besides, your father will be wearing his own at your bar mitzvah."

"Let me see, what else," Ma went on. She poured some more wine into her glass. "I must not forget the flowers, and I have to order a cake. Oh, God, and I promised to make hotel reservations for all the people from out of state. And I'd better start ordering food."

"Is it worth it, Ma?" I said.

"Huh?"

"Is it worth it? I mean, a woman has to be crazy to do all this."

"Oh, she does, does she?"

"Yeah," I said. "I mean, it's just not worth it, all this time and you're spending a fortune and I'm practically killing myself. For what? Just to prove I'm Jewish? I still think it's silly."

Ma smiled. "Well, maybe some day you won't," she said.

And then she kind of stared into her glass of wine for a

while and she said, "David, honey, you're not disappointed are you, that we can't have the reception in a hotel."

"No, Ma, that's okay," I said, even though I really was disappointed, "just as long as there's enough room to dance in."

"Oh, David," she said and she said it in a way that meant she knew something that I didn't know and that we both knew I wasn't going to like once I did know.

"Hit me with it," I said.

"There's not going to be any dancing, sweetheart."

I couldn't believe it.

"What are you talking about, no dancing?" I said. I pushed my chili bowl almost to the edge of the table. "Ma, the band is the best part of the reception. I told all my friends there would be a band."

"There can't be."

"Why not?" I shouted. I slammed my napkin down on the table. "Give me one good reason."

"It's going to be *Shabbes*," she said. *Shabbes* means it's the Sabbath, a holy day.

"Oh, great!" I said. "We certainly wouldn't want anybody having any fun on *Shabbes*."

"Oh, David, you can have fun. But there are no musical instruments allowed in the temple until after sunset. The reception will be over by then."

"Ma," I shouted, "What am I going to tell my friends?"

Ma sipped some wine, and then calmly said, "You're going to tell them that things have changed. That's what you're going to tell them."

"Changed? I'll say they've changed." I stood up quickly

93

and almost knocked my chair over. "Stupid bar mitzvah! Who needs it, anyhow."

"Honey, I'm sorry. There's nothing we can do about dancing now."

"Why didn't you tell me?" I said.

"I thought I did."

"Well, you didn't."

Ma was crying. Tears were falling into her bowl of chili, and I felt like the lowest worm that ever crawled across the planet.

"I know you're disappointed. So am I. I'm doing my best, honey. I'm just trying to make this day as special for you as I possibly can. There won't be a band and I'm sorry about that, truly I am, but it will still be nice, David, it will still be nice."

I didn't say a word. I didn't know what to say.

"But, oh, there's still so much more to do," Ma said. She kept wiping her eyes and the tears smudged all over her cheeks. "The house, I've got to fix it up. We'll be having people over that night and the next day. And then, shopping for all our clothes. Shirt. Tie. Shoes. My suit, Markie's suit. There's so much, honey. And then . . . then . . . David, honey, I know you're under a lot of pressure but please remember he . . . he's not just your grampa . . . it's *my father* who's dying."

Then Ma just started sobbing something awful, and all I could do was stand behind her and hug her for a while. I know it was the stupidest thing in the world to say but it was the only thing I could think of to say, so I said, "So why don't we just forget the whole thing. Cancel it."

94

Ma seemed to suddenly go limp then. "Ma," I said, "you know I didn't mean that."

I patted her shoulders the way she always pats mine when I don't feel so great, and then when she was starting to feel a little better I led her into the living room, to her easy chair where she likes to read at night, and sometimes fall asleep. She sat down and I told her to relax and I turned on the stereo to her favorite station, which only plays classical music.

"Thank you, honey," she said. She leaned back, wiping her eyes with a napkin.

I sat on the arm of the chair and just looked at her for a while. And I played with her hair. Ma likes that, when I play with her hair. And after a while her face started to get bright again and pretty and I could tell she was cooking up something in her brain.

"I've got it!" she announced.

"What?"

"David," she said. She leaned forward and took my hand. "I'll make a deal with you. If you find a band that's small enough to fit down the basement and smart enough to learn a couple of Jewish songs, then you can have them come here on Saturday night *after* your bar mitzvah reception. Then you and your friends can dance and have a great time. What do you say?"

"I say you're a genius!"

Ma was smiling again.

And so was I.

"David, my son, go get the wine please, and my glass." Ma looked very proud of herself, as if she had just landed the lead in her favorite play. "And David," she called when I was leaving the room, "bring an extra glass."

When I got back Ma set the two glasses and the bottle of wine down on the coffee table.

"Don't worry about the chili dishes, Ma," I said. "I'll wash them. I can play my haftorah tape while I'm getting dishpan hands."

Ma smiled. She picked up the wine bottle and filled her glass all the way to the top. And then she poured wine into the other glass, but just a little. She put down the wine bottle and handed me the glass. Then she picked up her own glass.

"*La Chaim!*" she said, which means "To Life!" It's a Jewish way of saying "Cheers" and "Good luck."

"*La Chaim!*" I said, and we sipped the wine.

# Chapter *14*

One good thing about being Jewish is that every time you turn around it's some kind of a holiday. In the fall we have Rosh Hashanah. In spring, it's Passover. And around December, there's Chanukah, which is great because it lasts for eight days and you get at least one present every single day. Chanukah usually comes right around Christmas, but it goes by the Hebrew calendar, so this year it started on the last day of November, at sunset, which meant that I was going to have an incredible month of December, presentwise. First, I'd get dozens of presents for Chanukah. Then for my bar mitzvah on December 17th, I'd get more presents, mostly money, which I'm supposed to put away for college. And the 17th is also my birthday, so there would be birthday presents. And then on Christmas, even though we're Jewish, Markie and I always get presents from friends who are Christians, like my Uncle Danny, and Jack and Carolyn Fogarty, who are friends of Ma's and live in St. Louis.

Of course being Jewish isn't all good. One of the bad things about being a Jewish kid is that it's a lot like being on a TV quiz show. There's always some adult around who says, "Hey, David, tell the Passover story," or "Hey, David, tell the Chanukah story," and you feel like the whole world is listening to see if you mess it up.

But at this Chanukah party I didn't have to tell the story. After Nana and Grampa and Uncle Danny and Aunt Nancy got to our house, carrying a bag of presents, and everybody wished everybody else Happy Chanukah about a hundred times, Nana raised a hand in the air for quiet and said, "Markie, my grandson, tell the Chanukah story."

Poor Markie. His face went red. I guess he had figured he'd done his bit for the Chanukah party by decorating the house. Markie had strung paper chains all over the place. He had even cut out paper draydles and menorahs, which are Chanukah symbols, and he had rigged this gigantic HAPPY CHANUKAH sign across the fireplace.

"Me?" Markie said. He was nervous and he looked at me because, even though Markie had told the story before, it was usually me who got stuck with the job.

"Markie," my father said, "don't you think David already has enough things to juggle?"

"I suppose," Markie said.

I knew how he felt. It's lousy when you get caught off guard like that.

"Well . . . it's about . . . um," Markie was stalling. "Let's see, the story of Chanukah is about . . ." He was starting to sweat. Everybody was listening.

Markie looked desperate. "King Antiochus and Judas," I mumbled, figuring I'd help him out. Besides, I was pretty anxious to get at the presents that were stacked in the corner of the living room and I was getting hungry for Ma's potato pancakes and knishes, which were out in the kitchen smelling delicious.

"Judas?" Markie said. "Oh, yeah. Maccabee. That was his name. Judas Maccabee." Then Markie went on to tell how the wicked King Antiochus led an army against Judas Maccabee and the Jews. In Jerusalem. In the olden days. "But the Jews won!" he said.

Markie was relieved, and I could see he was getting ready to sneak out of the room. But then Nana went over to him and wrapped her arms around him and said, "So tell me, darling, why were they fighting?"

"Huh? Because of . . ." He was stalling again.

Everybody waited for him to go on. Markie shrugged his shoulders. He looked to me and I could read his lips. "Help me."

"Do the temple part first," I said. "Then the oil."

Markie's eyebrows dipped and he looked down at his shoelaces. When he looked up he was smiling.

"They were fighting because Antiochus tried to stop them from praying in their temple. That's why. So they fought. And the Jews won."

"Good for you," Nana said.

"And then, when they got back to their temple," Markie went on, "they found a major mess."

Everyone laughed.

"Go on, my little *shmendrick*," Grampa said.

"So, they began to put everything back together, you know. And when they went to put oil in their lamp so they could see the Torah in order to study, well, they didn't have enough of it to burn for very long."

Dad interrupted. "That's right. Markie. So, what happened next?"

"So, they went out and searched all over the place for some more oil. But they only found enough to last for about a day."

Markie was on a roll by now. He knew he had the rest of the story in the bag. I was happy for him. It was almost over. It's hard when everyone's looking at you and expecting you to know all the right things to say.

While Markie was telling the rest of the story, I watched Max Levene. Grampa. He was sitting across the room from me, stretched out in Ma's easy chair. She always let's him use it when he's in our house. Grampa's eyes were closed and his lips were moving, but just slightly. I knew he was telling the Chanukah story along with Markie. I crept across the room while Markie was still talking and I sat on the arm of the chair. Grampa held my hand, but we didn't say anything. Being close to him like that, I could hear him telling the story softly. But I couldn't tell what he was saying because he was telling it in Yiddish, which is the language he spoke when he was a kid.

Markie finished the story by telling how, even though there was only enough oil to burn for one day, the oil lasted for eight days and eight nights. That's when Nana hollered, "A regular miracle, I tell you, it was a wonderful thing!" as if she had actually been there to see it.

I wanted to talk to Grampa then, but Dad said it was time to light the Chanukah candles. That's something you do every year. There are eight candles. On the first night you light one. On the second night you light two. And so forth. The candles are in this beautiful candleholder called a menorah, which is usually made out of silver or brass.

Dad gave me the matches. Markie and I put on our yarmulkes. And I lit the shammes candle. That's the one in the middle that you always use to light the others. Then Markie lit the candle for the first night and he and I sang the first blessing together. It goes, "BO-RUCH A-TO A-DO-NOI E-LO-HEY-NU ME-LECH HO-O-LOM, A-SHER KI-D'SHO-NU B'MITZ-VO-SOV, V'TZI-VO-NU L'HAD-LIK NER SHEL HA-NU-KAH," and it means, "Blessed art thou, O Lord, who has commanded us to kindle the Chanukah light."

When we finished that blessing Nana burst out with, "Happy Chanukah everybody!"

"Not yet, Nana," Markie said. "There are still two more blessings, remember?"

Everyone laughed.

"Oh, my, oh, my," Nana said. She put her fingers to her mouth. "You should excuse me. I'm very, very sorry."

When Nana gets so serious like that Markie and I start giggling. We nearly choked on our laughter, but somehow we got through the other two blessings. And then it was okay for everybody to say, "Happy Chanukah." Then everybody kissed and hugged everybody else. I guess that's a tradition, too, but nobody thinks about it. It just happens naturally.

I wanted to sit with Grampa then and tell him about

Kelly, and about the fact that I was going out for the eighth-grade basketball team and that the Midgets had finished in third place and I'd be in the play-off game against the Lancaster Gnats. But Ma started bringing in the latkes . . . that's potato pancakes . . . and knishes, and of course Nana had brought enough food to sink a battleship, so we all mostly just ate for a while.

Then it was time to open presents. I got a basketball from Uncle Danny and Aunt Nancy, and a savings bond from Nana and Grampa, and Ma and Dad gave me a ring and a new tape recorder. I told Markie he could have my old one and he carried on as if I had given him the Eiffel Tower, which was great because I had been too broke to buy him anything but a crummy plastic harmonica for Chanukah.

While everybody was opening presents I stayed near Grampa. But I didn't know what to say to him, and he didn't say anything to me. I was really uncomfortable. It was like standing next to a girl at a dance and not knowing whether you should say something to her or wait until she says something to you.

"So, how's my grandson?" Grampa finally said.

I said, "Good. Thanks. How are you?" Only it came out really formal, like I was talking to somebody I hardly knew.

"Good? Thanks? How are you?" Grampa repeated. "This is how you talk to Max Levene?"

"Sorry," I said. "It's just . . ." and I turned my back on him. It was hard to look him in the eye. Dad had made a fire, so I stood by the fireplace jabbing logs with this long metal poker we have.

After a minute Grampa said, "So, I hear you're a real *gansa k'naker* these days." That means, big shot. "A bar mitzvah boy who's got a girlfriend, yet!"

"You know about Kelly?" I said. I turned around.

Max Levene smiled. "Oh, I hear a few things," he said. "Tell me about this girlfriend."

"Well, she's not Jewish," I said.

"This is a tragedy?" he said. 'A lot of people are not Jewish. Is she pretty?"

"Oh, she's beautiful, Grampa. And she's smart. I want you to meet her. Only I hardly see her myself these days. I mean with studying my haftorah and everything."

"Yes," Grampa said. "It is very hard for a boy to study for his bar mitzvah. And it's even harder when there is a girl who is pretty and is smart that he would like to be with. I tell you the truth, grandson, I would rather be with a pretty girl than study the haftorah. But you don't have so long to go. Sixteen days, that is all."

"Yeah," I said, and I was wondering how many days Max Levene had to go.

"David," he said, "you see that box." He pointed to a present that hadn't been opened. "Bring it to me."

I picked it up. I couldn't believe how heavy it was. I handed it to Max Levene and he handed it right back to me. "It is yours," he said. "Happy Chanukah."

"For me? What is it?"

"Open it," he said.

I sat on the floor and ripped off the pretty wrapping paper. It was a cardboard box. I pulled it open and inside was the old safe that Grampa had kept in the wall, the one I used to keep my "Top Secret" stuff in. I couldn't believe it. When I was a little kid I used to pray every night that I'd have a safe like that someday.

"Oh, Grampa," I said. I gave him a hug. He didn't hug me back as hard as he used to. "This is great," I said. "I can keep my bonds in it and my ring and all my bar mitzvah stuff." I didn't say it, but I was thinking maybe Kelly would send me a love letter and I could put that in the safe so Markie wouldn't find it.

Grampa looked old and he looked tired, but his eyes shone like jewels. I could see that he was getting sleepy and would need a nap. But before he closed his eyes and leaned way back in the chair he said, "David, a safe is good to lock up your money and your secret stuff. But you listen to Max Levene. When you have feelings, David, those you don't keep in a safe, those you don't lock up. You know what I'm talking?"

"Yeah, Grampa," I said, "I know what you're talking."

# Chapter *15*

"Go for it!" Kelly shouted.

This was the day of the tryouts for the eighth-grade team, and I came dashing downcourt with the ball. When I heard Kelly shout I took a jump shot from the foul line. It went in.

"Way to go!" Randy cried. He and Kelly had both come to the gym to give me moral support.

On the next time downcourt I was wide open for a shot, but I didn't want to be a ball-hog, so I passed off to one of the other kids. He shot and missed and I zipped in under the basket and popped the ball in without getting blocked, which is unusual for such a short kid.

"Yay, David!" Kelly shouted. I should have been embarrassed, I guess, but I was having fun because I was doing so well. And besides, a few of the other kids had friends there, too.

The way the tryout worked was that Coach Bellarosa made the boys scrimmage in games of three-on-three. He kept substituting to see how kids played in different combinations. I was the shortest kid there but I was doing better than anybody. I had my outside shot working like a charm. I shot eight long bombs, and seven of them went in, and I picked up a couple of assists, and I only knocked the ball out of bounds once. Of course being so short I didn't do a whole lot of damage on the boards. On one of the breaks when I was sitting on the bench, the coach said, "David, go under the boards. I don't care if you don't get any rebounds as long as you're not afraid to go under the boards on defense and just wave your hands at your man." So I did that and I managed to steal the ball a couple of times.

When the scrimmage was over, Randy was all excited. "It's a great day for short people," he said.

"You were really wonderful, David," Kelly said.

"I think you did it," Randy said, "I think you made the team."

"No," I said, "I'm still pretty short next to those guys." But secretly, I was thinking I had a chance, a real chance.

Kelly kept telling me how wonderful I was and then she said, "Do you want to go someplace for a snack?"

"No," I said, "I can't."

"Oh," she said a little coolly, "any special reason?"

"I have a ton of homework tonight, plus all my bar mitzvah stuff."

Kelly folded her arms and glared at me for a minute. Then, she gave me a kiss on the cheek, said, "Call me," and turned to Randy and said, "Come on, Randy, let's go. We don't want to bother David. He's busy."

106

Kelly was mad. I could tell. And that night I should have called her. But I didn't. Everything was getting too important. I couldn't tell, just then, which important thing I cared about most.

Then a couple of days later it happened. It was, as Nana would say, "A regular miracle, that's what!" I made the team. Me. Short me. My name was on the bulletin board on a list of boys who were supposed to report to the gym after school. The notice didn't say that these were the kids who had made the basketball team. But everybody knew that's what it was.

I could only stay in the gym for a few minutes that afternoon because of Hebrew school. The coach told us we would get uniforms and we had to keep our marks up and there would be basketball practice twice a week. Then I raised my hand and told him I had to go.

"I talked to your father," he said before I left. "I know you're going to be pretty tied up until the 17th. Just try to make it to as many practices as you can."

I was so incredibly happy about making the team that I danced out to the parking lot.

I was still in shock when I got into Ma's car.

"I did it, Ma," I said. "I made the team."

"Oh, David," Ma shrieked, "that's fantastic. I'm so proud of you. You wanted it, you worked for it, and you did it. Congratulations."

And so I was an official member of the junior-high-school basketball team. And with my bar mitzvah coming at me like a meteor out of the sky, with my girlfriend mad at me, and my grandfather dying, and with a ton of homework and a haftorah and a *maftir* to learn and, on top of that, a Shrimp League playoff game coming up, I did what any normal person would do. I went crazy.

Really. I didn't think of it that way at the time, but I can see now that I went a little crazy. It was only for about a week, but it seems longer. I came home from Hebrew school every day and went to my room and stayed there like a hermit. I did my homework first, then I worked on my Hebrew stuff. I didn't talk to anyone. I just grunted. I still didn't call Kelly. And when Randy kept calling to plan strategy for the Midget's play-off game, I told Ma to tell him I was dead. She just told him I couldn't come to the phone right then.

Once, Ma dropped me off at the junior high after Hebrew school and I caught the tail end of basketball practice, and it was the only time I wasn't totally crazy. I didn't play great, but I didn't play horribly, either. Everything was getting to me. But mostly, I guess, it was Max Levene.

I knew Grampa was dying and I knew I couldn't do anything to stop it, but I still needed to talk about it. I wanted to make sure that Max Levene knew how I felt. And I hadn't really told him.

And then on the 12th, on the day of the playoff game, I did something weird. I'm not sure if I was still crazy or if I was getting sane again, but I'm sure Ma must have thought I was off my rocker, because I came out of school and got in her car and said, "Take me to Westboro," which is kind of funny because there's a mental hospital in Westboro, but that's not where I wanted to go.

108

"Westboro?" she said. "David, we have to go to Hebrew school."

"No," I said. "You have to take me to Westboro. There's a bus that goes all the way down Route 9 to Newton. I need to see Grampa."

"David, what for?"

"My suit," I said. It didn't make any sense but I figured it was the kind of reason Ma would understand.

"Your suit?"

"Yeah, my bar mitzvah suit. Grampa made my bar mitzvah suit, right, and I have to try it on."

"David, don't be ridiculous. I was going to get it for you tomorrow. Honey, you're acting strange."

"Ma, I have to see Grampa, that's all. I can take the bus from Westboro. It won't kill me to miss Hebrew school one day."

"Well, I don't know," she said.

"Ma, please, just take me to the bus stop."

"But tonight's your basketball game, honey."

"I'll be back in time. I'll call you from the bus stop. I just need to see Grampa for a while."

Ma looked confused but she could tell that I meant business. "David, if it's that important to you, I'll drive you to Newton."

"No," I said. "I have to go alone. I want it to be just me and Max Levene."

Ma didn't say anything for a while, but she started driving in the direction of Westboro. Then finally she said softly, "David, I know you're upset about what's happening to Grampa. But you don't have to go down there to tell him you love him. Grampa knows that. You've told him many, many times."

"I know, Ma, I know. It's not that."

"Then what? What's wrong?"

"It's hard to explain," I said.

"Try," she said.

"I have to tell him I'm Jewish."

"What? David, what . . .? He knows you're Jewish."

"No, Ma, he doesn't, not really. You don't understand."

We were almost to Westboro when Ma said, "I do understand, David. Really." She was crying. Ma's pretty good at driving and crying at the same time so we didn't crash into a tree or anything. When we got to the bus stop she said, "Call me when you're leaving Grampa's, so I can be here to pick you up."

After I got off the bus in Newton I had to walk about a half a mile to Grampa's house. It was a nice day for walking, though, not too cold, and the sun was shining. When I rang the bell Grampa came to the door. The wrinkles in his face curled into a big smile.

"Well, well, David," he said, "your mother called, said I should expect a distinguished visitor, and here you are. Come in, come in."

I followed Grampa into his living room. He sat on the couch and I looked around for Nana.

"You'll not be surprised to know your Nana is in the kitchen making you something to eat."

"Thanks," I said. "I'm not hungry."

"Hmmn," Max Levene said. "So why am I so honored today to have your company?"

110

"Oh, I just thought I'd come down and try on my bar mitzvah suit. Ma says it's finished."

"Your suit. Your suit!" Grampa's eyes lit up. "Yes, it's finished and it's a wonderful job if I do say so myself. But you didn't have to come down here. Your mother would pick it up for you while you're in school."

"Yeah, I know, but I thought I'd better try it on, you know, to see if you made one leg shorter than the other or anything."

"Yes, I see what you mean," Max Levene said.

Then he took me upstairs to the little den where he sews things and I got into the suit. Max had taken my measurements for it a while ago and it fit perfectly. And it was beautiful, light blue, with a vest and inside pockets and everything.

Slowly, Grampa got down on his knees and played with the cuffs while I stood in front of the mirror. "David, you've grown a little," he said.

"Huh?"

"Yes, I put a little extra in the cuff, thinking a boy would grow, and I was right." Then without looking up at me he said, "So you took a long bus ride for a suit. I never saw a boy who was so interested in clothes before."

"Well, it wasn't just that," I said.

"Oh?"

"I need to . . . talk to you," I said.

"About what?"

". . . Basketball."

"Basketball again?" he said. "You think I'm such an expert on basketball?"

"No, but . . . I need to talk to you, that's all," I said.

"Yes," Grampa said, "and we'll talk. First we pack up your bar mitzvah suit, and then we will go for a walk."

Whenever Max Levene and I want to go for a walk while Nana is cooking we have to sneak out of the house. That's because if Nana catches us she'll say, "Oy! You're going for a walk on an empty stomach?" and she'll make us eat first. So Grampa and I always sneak out and we always call it, "Secret Plan Number 82." Eighty-two is just the number we made up and we've been using it for years, and the secret plan is just that Grampa will find the best way to get out of the house without Nana seeing us, and I'll follow him.

So after Grampa packed my suit in a box, he said, "Okay, David, we must do Secret Plan Number 82."

We crept down the stairs and Grampa cocked an ear to see if he could hear Nana thumping around in the kitchen. He smiled. Then he very quietly opened the hall closet and pulled out his coat. He signaled me to stay on the stairway, then he tiptoed into the living room and came back with my jacket. "Remember," he whispered, "the enemy has many weapons of torture. Potato knishes. Kreplach. Blintzes. Potato pancakes." It was nice to see Grampa actually giggle. We sneaked out the front door. "Chicken soup," he whispered as we crept around the house, ducking when we came to windows, "bagels and cream cheese." Finally, we got to the back of the house where the kitchen is and we hunched down low and went into the woods.

Grampa and I went down by the stream. Grampa said it was a little chilly to just sit in one place, so we walked

112

slowly. Little webs of ice had formed near the edges of the stream and I liked the crunch they made when I stepped on them.

"So, what is this about basketball that your Grampa is to help you with?" Grampa said.

"Well," I said, "you know about the Shrimp League that Randy and I started."

"For boys who are short?" he said.

"Right. Well my team is the Midgets and tonight's their first playoff game."

"Playoff? What is playoff?"

"Well, Randy and I set it up so we'd have a playoff just like the professionals. The Midgets finished in third place and we're going to play against the Lancaster Gnats because they finished first. Then tomorrow the Northboro Guppies . . . they finished second . . . will play against the Sterling Elves. They finished fourth. And the winners of the two games will play each other for the first Shrimp League Championship. Except that it will be the last one for me, because we made a rule that nobody who's past the eighth grade can play in the Shrimp League."

"Hmmn. Sounds important."

"It is," I said.

"But your Ma won't let you play because you must study your Hebrew?"

"No, Grampa, that's not it. It's just that . . . well, I know you have to take it easy these days . . ."

"Yes, I do," he said.

"But . . . Uncle Danny is coming to the game tonight."

"Yes, yes," Grampa said, "your Uncle Danny is

*meshugge* for basketball. So of course he should go."

"Grampa, I want you to come, too. To see me play." I said. I guess until I said it, I didn't realize how important it was to me to have Max Levene see me play.

"Okay," he said.

"Okay? Just like that, okay?"

"Sure," he said.

"But I thought you didn't like basketball so much?"

Grampa smiled. "Basketball, I don't like so much, no, but my grandson? . . . Ah, him, I love."

I took his hand, and we walked back up the hill to the house. I still wasn't hungry, but Nana made me take a bag of goodies in case I found myself starving to death on the bus. I called Ma to tell her I was on my way. And then Max Levene and I stood out on the sidewalk in front of his house, and he handed me the box with my suit in it.

"So, you have a good trip on the bus," Grampa said, "and you should get your telephone fixed real soon."

"My telephone? What'cha talkin', Max Levene? There's nothing wrong with my telephone."

"Oh? I just didn't think you would come all the way here to invite your grandfather to a basketball game if you could telephone him."

"Well, I just wanted to . . . you know, to spend some time with you. The way we used to."

"Yes," he said. "You and me, we've had some good times. David, is there something else you'd like to say before you go?"

My heart started thumping as if I was running full court on a fast break. "Ma says I don't have to tell you I love you. She says you know that."

114

"Yes, David, I know this. And I love you, my grand-son. But still it is good to say it once in a while."

"I wish . . . I wish you weren't dying," I said. There. I had said it out loud. I felt like somebody had finally taken the bricks off my back.

"Hmmn." Max smiled. "To tell you the truth, David, I'm not so happy about it, myself. But this is how it goes. But, David, don't buy me no flowers yet, okay. I will take my time with dying. You know I don't like to rush into things."

Grampa and I just looked at each other's eyes for a while. I thought about the day down by the stream when he had talked about tradition and about his family. And I thought about all the stuff I wanted to tell him, that I understood what he was saying. I wanted to tell him that I wasn't going to throw twigs in the stream.

"Goodbye my bar mitzvah boy," he said. "I see you later."

"Sholem aleichem," I said, and I put my suit box down on the sidewalk so I could hug my grandfather.

"Aleichem sholem," he said, and I started walking for the bus.

# Chapter *16*

After Ma picked me up at the bus stop, I had to run around like crazy to get to St. John's gym on time. The game started at eight o'clock, and there were a lot more people than I expected. I mean it wasn't exactly the Boston Garden, but my parents came and Markie, and a lot of mothers and fathers of kids on both teams. And there were a lot of other kids, too, little kids mostly who like us because we're short. And my Uncle Danny was there with Max, and even Nana. And the O'Neils. Everybody sat on benches on both sides of the gym.

The game started off kind of dull. We'd miss a basket and then the Gnats would miss a basket. Then we'd knock the ball out of bounds on some stupid play that didn't work, and then the Gnats would knock it out of bounds. But in the second half, when we were four points down, I started getting a hot hand, mostly from outside, and so did Phil Clinton. We would have run up a pretty good lead except that the Gnats have got this kid, Bob Hayes, who can shoot jump shots better than Magic Johnson, and he started getting hot, real hot.

So when there was just ten seconds left in the game we were all tied up, 46–46. I figured we'd hold for one shot and if we didn't score we could go into overtime, anyhow. In a situation like that you always wait until there's just a couple of seconds left before you shoot. That way, even if you miss, the other team won't have time to get back downcourt and shoot. So I took the ball down, and the Gnats had two men guarding me, but I'm a pretty good dribbler, so they couldn't steal the ball. The plan was for Phil Clinton to get as close to the basket as he could, then get free with about three seconds left and I'd hit him with a pass. So I stayed way outside and I watched for him, and when there was three seconds left in the game he shook his man. I picked up the ball to pass to him, and my two men dropped off me to move toward the basket. But just as I was about to throw the ball to Phil, I saw his man jump right in front of him, so I held onto the ball, and there was one second left, and there was nothing else to do, so even though I was twenty feet away I shot the ball. It felt pretty good. It had a nice high arc and a lot of spin, which helps it stay straight. Then I heard the bell go off, which means there's no more time, and for a second the whole gym was as quiet as a graveyard. Then I heard a kid's voice shout, "It's good if it goes." It was Markie and he was standing up on one of the benches waving his hands in the air like a maniac. And then the ball started falling toward the basket. I knew with everybody being so short I didn't have to worry about anybody jumping up

lot of other clothes that I didn't need. And she got a suit for Markie, and some stuff for Dad and her. But Filene's didn't catch fire so I was sure that all the people who were coming from out of state to be at my bar mitzvah would somehow end up on the same plane and the plane would crash into a mountain. Either that, or the rabbi would break his leg for sure and he wouldn't be able to help me through the final week.

Rabbi Kauffman came over Wednesday evening. I had missed Hebrew school that day because Ma was running all over the place ordering flowers and food for the party we'd be having in our house on Saturday night after the reception. I was glad the rabbi came, because I needed the help. But I was also kind of not so glad because I figured if he came to the house he must have thought I was in a lot of trouble. And he was right. I was having trouble with my haftorah. I mean, I 'd chant it once and get it all right. Then I'd try again and I'd mess it up or get halfway through it and my brain would turn to absolute mush. Sometimes it would feel as if my brain was completely filled with as many thoughts as it could hold and when I tried to squeeze in one more they all got crushed. Mush. I was getting excited about my bar mitzvah. But, to tell the truth, I was also scared to death.

Anyhow, the rabbi came over and we sat in the kitchen with our books that start at the end and end at the beginning. I read and reread the prayers and blessings that I would have to lead in Hebrew. Then we went over some of the responsive readings, which wasn't so bad, since they were in English. Then I tried the *maftir* and I kept messing it up. Finally I got fed up with it and told the rabbi, "I can't do it."

And the rabbi said, "Yes, you can," and he told me to just work on the hard parts. And I have to admit, after a while I was starting to get it right every time. It was becoming obvious to me that I would do fine on my blessings and prayers and even on the *maftir*, but when it came to the haftorah, the most important moment for a bar mitzvah boy, I would make an absolute fool of myself. Then it was clear to me why there hadn't been any time bombs, or fires at Filene's. My haftorah was going to be the disaster.

Dad came in when I was chanting the *maftir* for the last time. I did it perfectly. I could picture myself standing up there on the *bimah* chanting the *maftir* right from the Torah just like a regular rabbi. There wasn't another kid in all of Westbridge who could do that. Certainly not Eddie Gould.

When that was done, Dad and the rabbi applauded and the rabbi was going to leave, but Dad said, "No. Wait a minute, Rabbi, I think you'll find this interesting."

He had a long box with him and he led us into the dining room and set the box down on the table. "David, my son, for you," he said.

"Ma says I'm not supposed to open my bar mitzvah presents until Saturday night at the party."

Dad grinned. "I think you'll need this a little before then," he said.

I pulled the top off the cardboard box. It was a blue *tallis*. I couldn't believe it. A sky blue *tallis*.

"*Ayzeh yo'fee!*" the rabbi said, which is probably Hebrew for "that's a real sharp *tallis*."

I gently lifted the *tallis* out of the box, as if I were carrying an injured bird. It was silky, and it flowed over my fingers like liquid.

"The Lower East Side," my father was saying. "Now that's where you can get a *tallis*!"

"You went all the way to New York," I said, "on a work day!"

The *tallis* had hand-embroidered symbols all over it.

"The twelve tribes of Israel," the rabbi explained. I started to pull it over my shoulders.

"No, David, wait," my father said. He smiled. "Saturday."

"Right," I said.

There wasn't much to say except, "It's beautiful," which I said about twenty times. And, "Thank you," of course. I wanted to hug Dad. And I thought for a minute he was going to hug me, but he just put a hand on my shoulder and patted me and said, "I'm glad you like it, son." Then he pulled back as if he'd suddenly remembered something, and his eyes lit up.

"Wait!" he said. "Something else," and he scooted out again. I had never seen my father so excited about something that wasn't happening on a ball field.

"From Grampa Harry," he said, when he came back in carrying a brown paper bag. "This was mine. From my own bar mitzvah."

I opened the bag and pulled out a yarmulke. It was obviously old, but it was fancy like the *tallis*, handmade and with a lot of decorations.

"Try it on, David," Dad said. "Let's see if it will stay on top of that mop of yours."

I stuck it on my head.

"It will be fine," he said, "but the bar mitzvah boy needs a haircut."

Before the rabbi left he went over the "ADON OLOM" with me and Markie. That's a song that we would sing together. Then he gave me a speech he had written for me. It was one of those form speeches with a list of all the people I should thank. Most kids probably read a form speech because there's just not time to write one when you're studying everything else. Having the speech was a relief, because I sure hadn't started to write one myself.

After supper that night I trudged upstairs to my usual treat of homework and Hebrew study, and I found my new tape recorder on my bed. On top of it there was a homemade greeting card, with all kinds of colorful pictures and stars. Obviously, the work of my little brother. I opened it. Inside the card it said, "Dear David, I made you a present. Just press 'Play.' Love, Markie." I pressed the "play" button.

First I heard the thumping of Markie on the piano, then the drum and the guitar so I knew it was Popcorn. I didn't know what was coming, but I could tell it was pretty lively. Then I heard Markie's voice sounding so happy the way it does when he sings. He sang a song that he wrote just for me and it went like this:

> *I've got a plan to try*
> *No need to cheat or lie*
> *To get the most out of my life*
> *And heaven knows . . .*
> *IT'S GOOD IF IT GOES*

*You helped me find a way*
*To juggle work and play*
*And get just what I need*
*But still succeed to grow . . .*
*IT'S GOOD IF IT GOES*

*Back when things got rough*
*And I felt like giving up*
*You were there*
*To say to me*
*Get off your butt*
*So you can see that . . .*

*In life we must take risks*
*And even if we miss*
*We'll get another shot*
*And if it's on the nose . . .*
*IT'S GOOD IF IT GOES*

After I played the song, I played it again. And again. And again. It was catchy. And besides, nobody had ever written a song for me before. I played it about ten more times that night and by the time I went to bed I knew it perfectly, which was more than I could say about my haftorah.

# Chapter *17*

By Thursday evening I was a very sick human being. "VA YIK R'VU Y'MAY DOVID LO MUS, VAI TSAV ES SHLO-MO V'NO LAY-MOR . . ." I kept singing, from memory, which is a pretty weird thing for a kid to be singing. But it's the first line of my haftorah. If you read it in English it would say, "Now the days of David drew nigh that he should die; and he charged Solomon his son." I kept chanting it over and over. By this time I felt I knew my haftorah perfectly, but I was convinced that when the moment came to say it in front of two hundred people I would have an attack of mush brain. So I stood in front of my mirror singing the first line. I thought of the first line as being like the end of a ball of string. If I could find that, I'd have the whole thing. I knew once I started my haftorah I'd be okay, everything else would follow.

When I was singing, "VA YIK R'VU Y'MAY DOVID LO MUS, VAI TSAV ES SHLO-MO V'NO LAY-MOR," for the ninety-fifth time, Markie came knocking on my door.

125

I opened the door and Markie stood out in the hallway.

"Hi, Mark!"

"Hi!" he said. He looked as if he was afraid I was going to pull a gun on him. I guess I hadn't been the easiest guy in the world to get along with lately.

"Ma says I should do anything I can to help you. Is there something you want me to do?"

"Yeah," I said.

"What?"

"Not now," I said. "I want you to do it on Saturday."

"What is it?"

"Do my bar mitzvah for me."

Markie grinned. "I wouldn't mind," he said. "I'd be a star."

Markie looked like he really wanted to help, so I told him to come in and help me go over the order of service. The rabbi had given me the order so I'd know when to do what, and when to just sit still and act as if I wasn't nervous.

"Okay," I told Markie, "you read off what's on this list and I'll tell you if I know it cold. If I do, check it off. If I don't, circle it."

"Okay," he said. He was beaming. You'd think he'd just been elected president or something. "First it says, 'Preliminary Service. David, responsive reading.'"

"Piece of cake!" I said. "That's in English."

"Next it says, 'David's *tallis*.' What's that mean?"

"Oh, that's Ma's idea. She wants Dad to sort of 'present' it to me. Then I'll put it on and the rabbi will explain it to everyone who isn't Jewish. Then Dad will sit down again."

"Check it off?"

"Sure," I said. "Another piece of cake."

"Okay. Now it says, '*Shakchrus*.'"

"Right. That's the next part of the service. What happens first?"

"'Open the ark,'" Markie read, "'take out the Torah.'"

"Good. That's where Max Levene gets called. He gets the first *aliyah*."

An *aliyah*, I should explain, is an honor. Different Jewish men get to do things during a service, like one will open the ark and another might hold the Torah or read a blessing.

"Is Grampa going to take out the Torah?" Markie asked.

"No, he's just going to open the ark. Then Grampa Harry gets called and then Dad. Grampa Harry will take out the Torah and hand it to Dad. Then Dad will hand it to me. It's supposed to be symbolic, you know, handing down the Torah from generation to generation. So keep your eye on Ma. She'll probably be crying. What's next?"

"It says, 'David, blessing and march with Torah.'"

"Right. I carry it down the aisle and the rabbi and Max Levene march down the aisle with me, and people kiss the Torah."

"They kiss it?"

"Well, they don't kiss *it*. They touch it with their fingers, or their prayer books, then they kiss their fingers or the books."

"Why do they do that?"

"It's just a tradition, that's all," I said.

"It doesn't make any sense," Markie said.

"Traditions aren't supposed to make sense, Markie," I

explained. "They're just supposed to make you feel good. Anyhow, people will have plenty of time to kiss the Torah because I'm going to be walking real slow. That Torah weighs a ton."

"Check it off?"

"Yeah, what's next?"

"It says, 'The Torah reading.'"

"That's when I get to sit down and worry for a while," I said. "All the men on the *aliyah* list come up one at a time and do the blessings during the Torah reading."

"Who's on the list?"

"Oh, you know, Uncle Alan, Mr. Wilkenfeld, people like that. There're about seven of them."

"Uncle Danny?"

"No, Ma and Dad couldn't put him on the list. You have to be Jewish. Besides, he'll be busy with his recording equipment. He's going to tape-record my bar mitzvah."

Markie checked off the Torah reading. "Next is, 'David, *maftir*,'" he said.

"Oh-oh, you'd better circle it," I said. "I still need to work on it."

"Next, it says, 'Blessing,' then, 'The haftorah.'"

"The biggie!" I said.

"Do you know it?"

"Yeah," I said, though I didn't sound real positive. "If I can get started, I know it. Markie, I want you to do me a favor."

"Sure."

"When it's time for me to chant my haftorah, if I go more than five seconds without starting I want you to

128

shoot me. It will be faster than slowly dying of embarrassment in front of two hundred people. What comes after the haftorah if I'm still alive?"

"It says, 'Responsive reading, prayer, English.'"

"Check it off."

"All of it?"

"Sure," I said. "The rest is easy. Once I'm past the haftorah it's all downhill. Next?"

"'Presentation of gifts.'"

"Check that off, old buddy," I said. "I'm getting something from the president of the temple, the president of the sisterhood, and the president of the local chapter of Hadassah. All I have to do is smile, say, "Thank you very much," and shake hands or get kissed maybe and take the presents. I think I can handle that okay, don't you?"

"Lucky!" Markie said.

"Your turn will come," I said. "What's next?"

"It says, 'Rabbi's address to bar mitzvah family.'"

"Check it off. What about my speech?"

"That's next."

"Okay," I said, "let me read it to you. See how it sounds."

"You wrote a speech already?"

"No," I said. "I didn't have to. The rabbi gave me one." I started reading to Markie. "Honored Rabbi, my dear parents, grandparents, relatives and friends. My appearance this morning to celebrate my bar mitzvah marks an important and significant event in my life and in the lives of my parents and grandparents. This is a sacred and solemn moment as I become initiated as a responsible member of my people, dedicated to the laws of our Torah

129

and dedicated to uphold and preserve its ideals. I am not unmindful of the responsibility which goes along with such an initiation. It would be . . ."

Right about then I heard this snoring sound. It was Markie. He had stretched out on my bed and closed his eyes, and he was making these loud snoring noises as if the speech had put him to sleep.

"That bad, huh?" I said.

"It's not bad," he said. "It just doesn't sound like you."

"Well, it will have to do," I said. "What's next?" I threw down the speech without reading the rest to Markie. "And put a circle around the speech," I said.

"The last thing is the 'Adon Olom,'" Markie said.

"Yeah, you and I have to lead it, so you'd better keep practicing it."

"I know it," Markie said. Then he made a face. "Sort of," he said. "I'd better put a circle around it."

I took the order of service back from Markie and I realized I was in better shape than I'd thought. The only things I needed to practice were the *maftir*, reading the speech and singing the "Adon Olom" with Markie. And my haftorah, of course. I'd still practice that every chance I got.

And that's what I was doing about an hour later when the phone rang. It was Kelly.

"David, what is the matter with you?" she said. She sounded angry.

"Nothing," I said. "What makes you think something's the matter?"

"Oh, I just thought something terrible must have happened since you were supposed to be here an hour ago and you're not." Now she sounded sarcastic.

"There?"

"Dinner," she said. "Remember? It's Thursday night."

"Ohmigosh!" I said. Right about then I was real glad that Kelly's hands were not anywhere near my throat. "I forgot. I . . . I . . . I'm sorry."

"You know, I've been working all afternoon to make you a lasagna dinner. And now it's just, just . . . sitting there cold." She started to cry, and I felt suddenly like the scum of the earth.

"Kelly, I really am sorry," I said. "I don't know, there were just so many things going on here, so many things I had to do for my . . ."

"Don't say it," she interrupted. "I know. For your bar mitzvah, right? Well, I've had it with your bar mitzvah, David. That's all you ever think about or talk about. You don't care about anything else, or anybody else!"

I couldn't believe this was happening. Kelly. Screaming at me. "Come on," I said, "that's not fair."

"*Fair?*" she shouted. She sounded like Ma. "I'll tell you what isn't fair. Asking me to go with you and then ignoring me, isn't fair. Making me cook dinner for a boy who doesn't show up and making me look like an idiot to my parents, that's not fair."

"But Kelly . . ."

"You're doing everything for everyone else," she said, "but you don't even have time to call me. That's not fair."

"But it's almost over," I said.

"Yes, well don't expect me to come running to you then

131

just because you've got some extra time. I'll tell you what I think of your bar mitzvah, David. I think it's dumb. All that time and money for nothing."

"It is not dumb!" I shouted.

"Yes, it is," she said. "You said so yourself."

"Well, I changed my mind," I said. "Okay?"

"Great!" she said. "Well, maybe I'll change my mind about a few things, too."

"Like what?" I said, but all I heard was the dial tone. Kelly had hung up on me. I tried to call her back, but the line was busy. She must have left the phone off the hook.

I was really mad at Kelly for calling the bar mitzvah dumb. I knew she didn't really mean it. It was me who she really thought was dumb. But I was mad, anyhow. I started pacing around my room like a maniac. Finally Markie came to the door. "What's wrong?" he said.

"What's wrong?" I sputtered. "I'll tell you what's wrong. It's . . . it's . . . this stupid speech," I said. I grabbed the speech the rabbi had written and I waved it in his face like a crazy man. "That's what's wrong."

"Oh," Markie said, and he left.

After he left I realized that the speech *was* wrong. It wasn't the only thing that was bothering me, but it was the only thing I could do something about. So I sat at my desk and wrote my own speech.

I wrote about how glad I was that all my grandparents could be there on my special day. I wrote about the great suit that Grampa Max Levene had made for me, and how much work he put into it. I wrote about how glad I was that so many people came from so far away just to see my bar mitzvah, and how lucky everyone was because they were going to taste Nana's fantastic cooking. And I wrote about Markie and I said I was lucky to have a little brother who would write a song for me, and I put in some stuff about the rabbi and how he must be a pretty great teacher if he could get me to learn all that Hebrew. And then at the end I wrote about Ma and Dad and how much I loved them and that even though studying for my bar mitzvah was a pain in the neck in some ways, I was lucky to have parents who would make me do it. By the time I was done writing, it was late and I was getting all choked up. I don't know if the speech was good or not, but it sure sounded like me.

133

# Chapter *18*

On Saturday I woke up at the ungodly hour of 4:30 even though my bar mitzvah wouldn't start until 9:00. The first thing I noticed was that I couldn't open my eyes. My upper eyelids had somehow gotten attached to the crusty edges of my lower lids. Stuck. I panicked. How could I possibly get through this day with stuck eyelids? I jumped out of bed, my heart racing. I stumbled to the bathroom, crashing into a hall table along the way, and I groped around for the water faucets. I turned them both on and started splashing water on my face. Nobody else was up yet. The house was silent except for the sound of running water and crust removal.

After I washed away all the crud, I took a deep breath and forced an eye open. It blinked. It saw. Good. Then the other eye. It blinked, too. O sight, I thought, what a wonderful thing. Then I took the hottest shower I could stand and when I got out, the mirror was all clouded up. I drew a heart on it and wrote, "David and Kelly."

Kelly, I thought, and my heart sank. I remembered

that things weren't so great with Kelly. The last sound I had heard from her was the crashing of her phone. And on Friday, I hadn't gone to school, so I didn't see her to make up. I wondered if Kelly would be at the temple. I wondered who else would be there, and right away I knew the answer: The whole world, that's who. Two hundred people. And every single one of them, all four hundred eyes, would be watching me.

What if I couldn't do it, I thought. What if something tragic happened? Like if my voice didn't work? After all, I thought, my eyes hadn't been working all that well just a minute ago. What if I opened my mouth and no sound came out? I'd be finished. Ruined. This day was so important to so many people that I was sure I'd wreck it. "Did you hear about David Newman?" people would say out on the streets, "Made a mess of the whole thing."

I had to test my voice. My parents were sleeping, and I knew if I woke Markie he'd probably whack me over the head with Ike, his giant stuffed bassett hound, and with my luck I'd probably be rushed to the hospital with some kind of brain injury. So instead I went back to my room. I grabbed my haftorah and began to chant softly. My voice! I heard it. Another close call, but the bar mitzvah would go on after all.

After I'd been chanting for about half an hour, there was a gentle knock on the door. I opened it. My father stood there in his pajamas.

"What are you doing?" he whispered.

"I'm going over my haftorah," I whispered back. "Did I wake you?"

"No," he whispered. "Couldn't sleep." Then he put his

135

arms out and pulled me close to him and he hugged me and whispered, "I just want you to know that I am very, very proud of you." Then he stumbled back across the hall to get a little more sleep.

It took me an hour to get dressed, and by the time I finished, everybody else was downstairs poking around in the kitchen. Actually it only took me about ten minutes to put on my suit, shirt, socks and everything. The rest of the time was spent wrestling with my necktie. The necktie was winning. No matter how I turned it, twisted it or yanked it, it always ended up looking like a pig's knuckle. Finally I stomped out of my room and ran to the head of the stairs and screamed, "*Help*."

Dad came to my rescue. It took him about three seconds to get the tie the way I wanted it. Then I went downstairs to the kitchen and Ma got mushy about the whole thing.

"Oh, David," she cried. "Today you are a man. A beautiful young man," and she kissed me.

"Ma! I am not a beautiful young man," I said. "I am a handsome young man."

"Right," she laughed. "Handsome. And you are, David. You are so handsome you are beautiful."

"Ma!"

"Never mind. Sit down and eat. And stop pacing."

Nobody was hungry, really, so we all sat around the table gnawing at the edges of toast until Ma said, "Okay, let's go over everything. Michael! Is everything ready for the party tonight?"

"Yep. Food's all here. Bar's set up. Everything looks good."

"David! You're sure the band knows how to get to the house?"

"They'll be here," I said. "If not, Popcorn will play, right Markie?"

"Michael! You have David's *tallis* and your own?"

"Check."

"Markie, do you have the 'ADON OLOM?'"

"Yes," Markie said.

"Gentlemen! Do you have your yarmulkes?"

We all said yes.

"Good," she said. "The yarmulkes for everybody else are at the temple. I left them there. One less thing to worry about."

"And don't forget the speech," Dad said. "David, do you have your speech and your haftorah and everything else you'll need?"

"Yes."

Then everyone finished their dressing or washing or whatever, while I just hung around, half panic-stricken. Before we got ready to leave I took the blue *tallis* from Dad and went upstairs. I put it around my shoulders and I put on my yarmulke and stood in front of the mirror to see how I'd look up there on the *bimah*. I looked, I have to admit, wonderful. And also, I didn't have to wonder any more whether or not I looked Jewish. I did.

When we were all downstairs again, everyone just stood still for a minute, staring at each other. We were in this together.

"Well?" Ma said.

"Well?" Markie said.

"Well?" I said.

"Let's do it," Dad said, and we were on our way.

I sat in the front seat with Dad because I was the bar mitzvah boy, and the drive went pretty smoothly until Ma started shrieking in the back seat.

*"Mack Mitchell's Pub?"* she screamed. *"Mack Mitchell's Pub?"*

"Huh? What about it?" Dad said, as we passed the restaurant and took a left.

*"Mack Mitchell's Pub,"* she said, pointing at the restaurant. "That place is called Mack Mitchell's Pub." She gaped at it as if it had just landed from outer space.

"Right," Dad said, "it used to be the Wayside Restaurant."

"Oh, God!" Ma said. "I knew something like this would happen. I knew something would go wrong. So we don't have a blizzard. We have . . . this."

"What on earth is wrong?" Dad said.

"Mack Mitchell's Pub, that's what's wrong. I can't believe it! Why didn't somebody tell me? I don't go this way anymore. I found a shortcut."

"Tell you what?" Dad sounded worried, like maybe he'd have to drop Ma off at a mental institution before we went to the temple.

"That the Wayside Restaurant was gone. That it changed it's name! Don't you see, honey. Nobody's going to find the temple. I sent all the out-of-town people a map. I told them to take a left at the Wayside Restaurant, the big red sign. Only there isn't any big red sign. They'll all get lost."

138

Ma whimpered for a while in the back seat and Dad tried to convince her that people would find the temple easily. But we all knew that getting lost in Fitchburg was as easy as putting on socks, and that a lot of people would miss a lot of the service while they were driving around looking for the Wayside Restaurant.

"*A drug store!*" Ma finally screamed.

"Oh, hon, do you have a headache?" Dad said.

"No, I don't have a headache. I have an idea. A drug store will be open at this hour." Then she thrust her arm out over the front seat as if she were the queen of Romania or something and she commanded, "Take me to a drug store."

When we finally found a drug store that was open, Ma rushed in and came out about twelve seconds later with a big pad of paper, a couple of magic markers and some masking tape. Dad drove us back to the corner where the Wayside Restaurant used to be and by the time we got there Ma had drawn three big signs that said, DAVID'S BAR MITZVAH, and they all had a bunch of arrows pointing to the right street. She jumped out of the car and ran around taping the signs. She taped one to a telephone pole, one to a street sign and one to a car that was parked on the corner and which, I guess, she figured would be there for a while. Then she got back into our car, saying, "Mack Mitchell's Pub, indeed! That will show them," and we were on our way once more.

# Chapter 19

We walked through the temple doors at a quarter to nine. It was very quiet. You know, the kind of quiet it is just before a bomb goes off. The rabbi greeted us. He was smiling . . . probably because he didn't have to chant the haftorah today. He had me to do it for him.

"*Mazel tov*," he said, which means, "congratulations." There was a whole bunch of handshaking. Ma thanked the rabbi for teaching me everything, then she threw me one of those "I'm so darned proud of you" smiles that she'd been giving me every ten seconds since breakfast.

"The boy . . . soon to be a man . . . was an excellent student," the rabbi said. Then he turned to me. "So, how is the bar mitzvah boy today?"

"Fine," I gulped.

"Not nervous?"

"What's to be nervous about?" I said. "It's only the most important day in my life, with the whole world watching. Nothing important."

"Good, good," the rabbi said, "then you'll do fine."

Then Ma said, "The *kiddush!*" and scurried downstairs. The *kiddush* is a buffet that you have at temple after every service . . . mostly wine and sponge cake . . . and when there's a bar mitzvah, the bar mitzvah family is in charge of the *kiddush*, too, so Ma had to go help set it up.

We went into the synagogue. I followed the rabbi up to the *bimah*. The synagogue was still empty, and except for a lot of flowers, it was the same as it always is. But it felt different to me. A lot different.

"Look what is here for you, David," the rabbi said.

He pointed behind the reading table. He had put an apple crate there, upside down.

"For me to stand on?"

"That's right," he said. "Now, when you chant your haftorah even people way in the back will get a good look at you."

I stood on the apple crate just to make sure it didn't wobble. It made me feel tall.

"So, my boy, are you ready?" the rabbi said.

"Yes," I answered.

"Then you should have a seat," he said. He handed me a siddur, which is a prayer book, and pointed me to a fancy, high-backed chair on the *bimah*. That's where the bar mitzvah boy sits and watches his whole life pass before his eyes like a condemned prisoner.

Pretty soon people started coming in. Mostly people I didn't know, at first, just the regular Jewish people coming for the *Shabbes* service. The rabbi told them what page to turn to in the siddur, and he started reading. The service is about three hours long, so most people don't come for the whole thing, and it's okay for people to just come in whenever they feel like it.

After the rabbi had been reading from the prayer book for about ten minutes I started to get really tense, and in my mind I made a list of all the things that would probably go wrong. There were about twenty people there, but I didn't recognize any of them except Ma and Dad and Markie, who were all sitting in the front row. They looked as nervous as I felt. Then Bill and Wanda Cartlan came in. They're friends of my parents', and they live in Westbridge. They waved to me, and I waved back. Then some more Westbridge people came in and sat down. The rabbi just kept reading. Then Uncle Phil and Aunt Sylvia showed up, and some people from Newton, and some of Ma's theater friends. And Coach Bellarosa. As they took their seats they looked like tourists in a foreign country the way they gaped at everything. My heart was going like crazy now. I clutched my siddur and my hands were all sweaty.

Next came my cousin Steve, who's about twenty-five, and his girlfriend, Anita, who looked delicious. Looking at Anita reminded me of Kelly, and I couldn't see her anywhere. I figured she must still be mad. Then, while I was sitting there trembling and hoping no one was noticing, my grandparents from New York came in. They threw me a big kiss, then they went down and sat with my parents and everyone hugged. The rabbi just kept reading. I guess everything seemed normal to him. Then some more Westbridge people came. Even the police chief, would you believe? And the tree warden! Then Randy and his parents came in with a whole bunch of the

Midgets and they all waved and gawked at everything as if they were getting a tour of the Celtics locker room. By the time they settled down, there were more than a hundred people there. They kept coming. The rabbi kept reading. And I kept trembling.

After a while the flow of people stopped. Almost everybody who could be there *was* there. But not Kelly. And then I realized suddenly that Grampa wasn't there, and Nana and Uncle Danny and Aunt Nancy. Ohmigosh, I thought, and I knew in an instant what had happened. Uncle Danny and Kelly's father had somehow crashed into each other, and everybody had been rushed to the hospital. Then I thought, no, it wasn't that. It was Grampa. It was his heart.

Before I could think of any more horrible things, I heard the rabbi say, "And now, I call upon David, who will lead the responsive reading."

I stood up. I walked to the table on my shaky legs. I read. I felt better, just *doing* something.

When I got back to my seat Nana and Max Levene were slowly walking down the aisle, with my aunt and uncle behind them. They didn't seem to have any injuries. Nana took one look at me and said right out loud, "Oy, would you look at my grandson. Such a beautiful boy, I'm telling you." Everyone laughed because she said it loud enough for the whole temple to hear. In fact, she said it loud enough for all of Fitchburg to hear.

"Nana!" I said under my breath while I was turning six shades of red, but all that did was make everybody laugh again.

Pretty soon the rabbi called my father up to the *bimah,*

and Dad presented me with the beautiful sky blue *tallis*. Everyone went, "ooh," and, "ahh," over it while Dad returned to his seat. After a while, Max Levene slowly came up the steps to the *bimah*, and Grampa Harry and my father followed him. They all smiled at me. Grampa Max opened the Ark. Grampa Harry took the Torah out and handed it to Dad, and then Dad handed it to me.

I proudly carried the Torah down the aisle and back again. While people kissed it, I looked around for Kelly. She wasn't there. And I guessed she wasn't coming. When the Torah was uncovered and open to be read, the other men who had *aliyahs* came up. Each sang the blessings and I could see that they were as nervous as I was, and had been practicing so they wouldn't mess up, either.

I was almost calmed down and then I heard the rabbi sing, *"Dovid Shmoiel ben Moshe."* Ohmigosh, that's me, I thought, and I jumped up. That's my Hebrew name and it means "David Scott, son of Michael." It was time for the last *aliyah* and the reading of the *maftir*.

I stepped up on my apple crate behind the reading table and the rabbi touched my spot in the Torah with his silver pointer. I touched the corner of my *tallis* to the spot, then I lifted the *tallis* to my lips and kissed it. That's what you do to show respect for the Torah.

My heart was beating fast, but my brain seemed to be working okay. It hadn't turned to mush. Yet. First I sang the blessing that all the men had sung.

Borchu es a'donoi hamvorach.

Bor uch adonoi hamvorach l'olom vo-ed

Boruch atto adonoi, elohenu melech ho'olom

144

ASHER BOCHAR BONU, MIKOL HOAMIM,
V'NOSAN LONU ES TOROSO.
BORUCH ATTO ADONOI NOSAIN HATORAH.

I cleared my throat. The Rabbi whispered, "Don't worry, David. If you get lost I am right next to you and I'll help you find your way again. Go ahead. You'll do fine."

I chanted the *maftir* perfectly. Which could only mean one thing. My haftorah would be a disaster. I sang the closing blessing, and then after the Torah was raised and it was tied and covered, I went back to my seat, which was starting to feel more and more like it was falling into a pit. I took a deep breath.

I stared out at the audience. Ma smiled at me and she mouthed the words, "Good Luck," probably because my haftorah was coming next and she knew that my legs were turning into jelly. I looked at Dad, too, and he smiled, and Markie smiled. I think mostly they smiled because they were so glad it wasn't them up on the *bimah*. Then I looked at my grandfather. Max Levene. He wasn't looking at me. He was staring into the siddur on his lap and I wanted him to be looking at me. I tried to send out telepathic messages with my mind. Look at me, I thought, look at me. But it didn't work. He didn't look up. My mouth suddenly went dry. I began to twitch. And I could feel it, my brain was turning to mush. I had chanted the *maftir* too well, and now I was going to pay for it. I tried to clear my throat and I couldn't even do that.

Look at me, Grampa, I thought. Look at me. I need you. I'm scared.

"And now," the rabbi was saying, "it is my great pleasure to call upon the bar mitzvah boy, David, to come and stand before you as he chants his haftorah. The haftorah for this *Shabbes* is from the second chapter of One Kings. David?"

I took one long enormous breath and stood up. Someone began clapping, then stopped suddenly. I looked out. It was Kelly. She was there. Our eyes met and she winked at me. I realized that I hadn't seen her before because she was so short. Like me. I'd have someone special to dance with, after all, I thought. Then I walked to the reading table and stepped up on my apple crate and braced myself for disaster.

I stared at my haftorah and tried to find a way to open my mouth. I waited. And I waited. I wondered if Markie had a gun with him. Then I looked up and over to Grampa Max Levene. This time he was looking right at me. His eyes shone and his gaze was steady. He nodded his head just a bit. It was his way of nudging me to begin. So I opened my mouth.

My voice. I heard it. It worked. I chanted the blessing. And then I looked out at the two hundred people and sang for them, "VA YIK R'VU Y'MAY DOVID LO MUS, VAI TSAV ES SHLO-MO V'NO LAY-MOR."